This book should be returned to any branch of the
Lancashire County Library on or before the date shown

Kelly ANS 0 6 SEP 2017 Platt 2 4 JAN 2020	- 4 AUG 2018 1 9 OCT 2019 1 3 APR 2018 17 OCT 2 8 DEC 2018	- 9 AUG 2019 2 2 AUG 2019 - 1 DEC 2020

Lancashire County Library
Bowran Street
Preston PR1 2UX

Lancashire
County Council

www.lancashire.gov.uk/libraries

LL1(A)

D1100712

30118119045130

SPECIAL MESSAGE TO READERS

THE ULVERSCROFT FOUNDATION
(registered UK charity number 264873)
was established in 1972 to provide funds for
research, diagnosis and treatment of eye diseases.
Examples of major projects funded by
the Ulverscroft Foundation are:-

- The Children's Eye Unit at Moorfields Eye
  Hospital, London
- The Ulverscroft Children's Eye Unit at Great
  Ormond Street Hospital for Sick Children
- Funding research into eye diseases and
  treatment at the Department of Ophthalmology,
  University of Leicester
- The Ulverscroft Vision Research Group,
  Institute of Child Health
- Twin operating theatres at the Western
  Ophthalmic Hospital, London
- The Chair of Ophthalmology at the Royal
  Australian College of Ophthalmologists

You can help further the work of the Foundation
by making a donation or leaving a legacy.
Every contribution is gratefully received. If you
would like to help support the Foundation or
require further information, please contact:

THE ULVERSCROFT FOUNDATION
The Green, Bradgate Road, Anstey
Leicester LE7 7FU, England
Tel: (0116) 236 4325

website: www.foundation.ulverscroft.com

TROUBLE IN PARADISE

When Kat's mother, Ruth, tells her that her home and shop are under threat of demolition from wealthy developer Sylvester Jordan, Kat resolves to support her struggle to stay put. So when a mysterious vandal begins to target the shop, Sylvester — or someone in his employ — is their chief suspect. However, Sylvester is also offering Kat opportunities that will support her struggling catering business — and, worst of all, she finds that the attraction she felt to him in her school days is still very much alive . . .

SUSAN UDY

TROUBLE IN PARADISE

Complete and Unabridged

LINFORD
Leicester

First published in Great Britain in 2016

First Linford Edition
published 2016

Copyright © 2016 by Susan Udy
All rights reserved

A catalogue record for this book is available
from the British Library.

ISBN 978–1–4448–2877–1

Published by
F. A. Thorpe (Publishing)
Anstey, Leicestershire

Set by Words & Graphics Ltd.
Anstey, Leicestershire
Printed and bound in Great Britain by
T. J. International Ltd., Padstow, Cornwall

This book is printed on acid-free paper

119045130

1

The figure stood motionless, staring at the fronts of the only two shops that were still occupied in the row of ten that lined one side of Paradise Road, all of which were scheduled for demolition. One was a florist's, Petals; the other was Charlie's DIY.

It was impossible to distinguish any identifying features. The long, dark overcoat and wide-brimmed hat pulled low over the face guaranteed that. Together, they bestowed total anonymity.

Suddenly, an arm lifted and a brick flew through the air to crash noisily into the glass of the florist's window. A spider web of cracks instantly appeared and a cascade of glass splinters dropped inside, liberally sprinkling the flowers on display in the window.

A light went on and a woman's face

appeared at an upstairs window as she stared down at the perpetrator of the damage. But she could barely have had time to register what was happening before whoever it was had swung and dashed along the road, coat flaring out behind, to disappear around a nearby corner.

The woman in the window moved back into the room and also disappeared from view.

★   ★   ★

It was the musical tones of her mobile phone that woke Kat Lucas from her deep sleep. She lifted her head from the pillow and squinted at the clock that sat on her bedside table. It was one thirty a.m. She groaned and stretched out an arm to grope for her phone.

'Yes, who is it?' She made no attempt to read the caller ID on the small screen, mainly because her eyes were refusing to focus properly. In fact, she could barely keep them open.

'Kat, it's me, Mum.'

Kat propped herself up on an elbow. 'Mum? What's wrong?' Her mother would never ring at this time unless there was some sort of emergency.

'Oh, Kat,' she wailed, 'someone's just heaved a brick through the shop window. Thank goodness I couldn't sleep and heard it.'

Kat sat up fully now, her tiredness thrust to one side. She swung her legs out from beneath the duvet. 'Have you rung the police?' She made a grab for the clothes she'd discarded only an hour or so previously.

'Of course I've rung the police. They're sending someone round. Will you come — please? I need you.'

Kat pulled on the skirt and blouse that were lying on the floor, precisely where she'd flung them just a short time ago. She wasn't normally this untidy, but she'd been too exhausted to do anything else with them. She'd been on her feet for most of the day and all evening, working, and all she'd wanted to do on arriving back at her flat was to collapse into bed. But now, mindful of the fact that it was the middle of October and the nights were growing cooler, she grabbed a sweater from a drawer and pulled it on over the blouse. Not that she minded that summer was over. In fact, she positively welcomed it.

Autumn meant the beginning of the dinner party season, hopefully. Her business, Katering For U, had been struggling for the past five months, people not seeming to want food prepared and cooked in their own homes by someone else. Not surprisingly, she supposed; it had been an unusually hot summer and barbecues had been the favoured method of entertaining guests. However, last evening she had single-handedly catered for a dinner party for ten, during which she'd managed to discreetly hand out several of her business cards in the hope that they would bring in future work. By the time she'd finished she'd been exhausted. Still, if her mother needed her she'd go, and that was that.

Ruth lived on the opposite side of Market Linford, in the flat above her shop, Petals. As it was only a mile or so from Kat, she was parking her van outside within a couple of minutes. A swift glance showed two policemen already with her mother. Another glance located the damage done to the window. The glass wasn't totally smashed, but it was very badly fractured.

She opened the shop door and went in. The policemen swung to look at her. She recognised one of them, Paul Taylor. They'd been at school together, though not in the same year; he was older by a couple of years. They'd known each other for most of their lives.

'Hi, Kat,' he greeted her.

'Hello, Paul. What's the damage?'

'Well, just what you can see: a cracked window. It appears no one actually got inside.'

'Good.' She went and inspected it. 'We'll have to put something over it temporarily, just till morning. Then get it repaired.'

'If you've got an old cardboard box, you can flatten it out and — you know what, I'll do it for you.'

Once they'd finished and gone, Kat asked her mother, 'I know you told the police you saw someone, but tell me again. I was busy inspecting the window and didn't hear all the details.'

'Well, someone was standing on the pavement. I only saw whoever it was for a second. It was him, wasn't it? Sylvester Jordan,' Ruth burst out. 'Either him or that awful sidekick of his, Brett someone — Brett Sinclair, that's it. Hard as nails, he looks. He was the one who approached us all initially with the offer to buy. I wouldn't trust him as far as I could spit,' she snorted angrily. 'Which isn't very far. He's built like a tank.'

'Did it look like either of them?'

'I couldn't tell. Couldn't make out much at all, as a matter of fact. It all happened so quickly. He saw me looking down and ran off. It has to be Sylvester Jordan, or someone who works for him. He's determined to get me out. Well, I've got news for him. I'm not going — and neither is Charlie.'

'I didn't notice — is Charlie's window damaged too?'

'No, just mine. Me catching him in the act obviously scared him off.'

'So you weren't able to identify whoever it was?'

'No. He wore a long coat and a wide-brimmed hat pulled down over his face. A very effective disguise. Crafty beggar.'

'So you don't really know whether it actually was Sylvester Jordan or his man?'

'Of course it was one of them,' Ruth burst out. 'Who else could it be? Who else wants me out?'

'It could have been just a bit of vandalism. A local lad, bored and intent on a spot of mischief.' But, she thought, why would whoever it was bother to disguise his appearance in such an

7

elaborate way? He'd just wear a hoodie, wouldn't he? That was the usual garb for youthful troublemakers. In which case, Kat conceded that Ruth could be right; logic did seem to suggest it was Sylvester Jordan behind it. The disguise thing was a bit too sophisticated for the average youth simply up to no good.

Sylvester Jordan was a developer, and owner of Jordan Enterprises. He'd bought up all the other shops on the block and was planning to demolish them and erect an exclusive two-floor department store. His reasoning was that it would bring jobs and wealth into what was an increasingly rundown area of the town. According to him, it was all for the sake of the community.

Yeah, right, Kat silently scoffed now. *Nothing to do with making massive amounts of money.*

The trouble was, the local council planning committee was also backing him. In fact, the way she'd heard it, he'd already been given the nod to go ahead as soon as each of the premises was vacated. Which meant all that was stopping the demolition and the new building being constructed was the stubborn resistance of Ruth and her neighbour, DIY shop owner Charlie Turnbull. They were neither of them young people — Ruth being fifty-six, and Charlie a bit older than that — so if the culprit had been either Sylvester Jordan or Brett Sinclair, then sustained vandalism was going to be the name of the game. How long could they hold out against that?

However, Kat couldn't honestly envisage Sylvester Jordan throwing bricks through windows, in disguise or not. The most likely probability was that if Sylvester Jordan was connected to this, he would have paid someone else to do it.

Kat remembered him clearly from her schooldays. Like Paul, he'd been a couple of years older than her. In fact, if her memory served her right, Paul and Sylvester had been in the same year, if not the same class. She cringed as the memories flooded back, the main one being her gigantic crush on Sylvester. She laughed with scorn now at her own naivety.

She hadn't been alone, though; almost every other girl in the school had felt the same way. So in her juvenile view, she'd had plenty of justification for her girlish infatuation — and he'd been the handsomest boy in the entire school. Tall, even then approaching six feet, he had hair the colour of dark chocolate, and silvery-grey eyes that would darken to the colour of wet slate as he seemed to look straight through you. She also recalled his mouth. It had a decidedly sensuous look to it, mainly because of the full lower lip. His jaw line was chiselled, just like the heroes of the romantic novels she'd devoured in those days, and his nose was pure Grecian. He was magnificent.

Not that he'd ever noticed Kat, not even when her dewy-eyed gaze lingered on him, her longing clear to anyone who took the time to look. She'd thought he hadn't noticed, until one day — she'd been coming up to her fifteenth birthday — he had looked her way, and it hadn't been just a fleeting glance. It had, in fact, been long enough to inspire one of his friends to ask, 'Seen something you like?'

To which he'd swiftly looked away and scornfully said, 'Are you kidding? I like my women a bit more mature and with a bit of glamour.'

Thoroughly humiliated, Kat blushed a deep crimson and rushed away. That evening she'd stood in front of a mirror in her bedroom and closely scrutinised herself, trying to view herself through Sylvester's eyes. What she'd seen had filled her with despair.

She was modestly attractive, she supposed, in a mousy sort of way. The trouble was, her figure had barely developed, and she had small breasts that simply didn't show beneath her bargain-bought and plainly fashioned clothes. Which had been even more dispiriting, because it had become clear to her ever-watchful gaze the sort of girl

11

Sylvester favoured: the busty, curvaceous sort. Of course, in the fifteen years since then she'd developed a curvy figure of her own. And that, along with her shoulder-length honey-coloured hair, her heart-shaped face and high cheekbones, her hazel eyes that could in a certain light look pure green, and her full, naturally rose-tinted lips, attracted many an admiring stare. Her legs also came in for their fair share of attention. They were slender but shapely — in fact, she considered them her best feature.

But Sylvester's scornful words, all those years ago, had transformed her. From then on, she'd made much more of an effort — well, as much of an effort as her parents had been able to afford at the time — to make the most of what she had. She began to choose clothes that fitted her better and flattered her small breasts; she applied subtle touches of eye shadow and blusher. Nothing too obvious — she was at school, after all, and she didn't want the teachers to notice and send her home to clean it off, which had happened to one of the girls in her class.

But whatever she did, whatever lengths she went to, it made no difference. Sylvester simply didn't notice. In fact, he hardly ever glanced her way; and when he did, she wasn't sure he was really seeing her. In the end, she'd simply given up. He was never going to be attracted to her, not in a million years.

So it had been something of a relief when, at the age of eighteen, he'd left school to go to university, after which — or so she'd heard on the local grapevine — he'd started his own business. Now, at the age of thirty-two, he was well on his way to becoming a multi-millionaire; his wealth, according to a recent newspaper article about him, accumulated through a series of very profitable enterprises. He had interests in all sorts of concerns, and now owned a large building company, a nationwide chain of sports centres and spas, and a group of engineering companies. He was also the driving force behind several takeovers of seriously ailing companies, improving their performances and profitability with a view to reselling them for an even greater profit. His most recent acquisition had been an international IT company. Clearly, there was no limit to his talents.

The article had then gone on to detail his personal life, and it seemed that he'd also found time to get married, have two small sons in fairly quick succession, get divorced, and then, quite recently, return to Market Linford. Once there, he swiftly acquired a big house — a manor house, actually, that had once belonged to the Linford family — two miles outside of town; a house, moreover, that had acres of land, thus ensuring total privacy for himself and his sons. So, Kat now mused, with all that success to his name, why the hell couldn't he leave the small people

14

alone, people like Ruth and Charlie?

Anyway, his life had evidently changed so dramatically in the last fourteen years that she was quite sure he'd still barely glance her way. At the age of thirty, the mousy looks had vanished, as had the plain, unflattering clothes. Not that she'd bought anything for herself in months, such a parlous state were her finances in. She could still hold her own, though, whoever she was mixing with. A judicious use of the right accessories bestowed new vigour and style to an older outfit. And all of this, added to the fact that she now had her own business, meant her self-confidence had grown exponentially — or had done until things took a turn for the worse a few months ago. Now she was struggling to keep her head above an ever-increasing sea of debt, due solely to the downturn in her business, Katering For U.

In any case, she was unlikely to mix in the same circles as he did, so she doubted that they'd ever encounter each other. Not that she cared anymore whether he noticed her or not. She was long over Sylvester Jordan.

In the end, seeing how nervous her mother was after what had happened, Kat stayed the night with her, sleeping in the guest bedroom, a tiny room with just enough space for a single bed and a chest of drawers.

Ruth had moved from the family home four years ago in the aftermath of her husband's sudden heart attack and subsequent death. The proceeds from the sale of the relatively large detached house had been enough to buy the small flower shop and leave some money left over. After which, Ruth had set about creating a new life for herself, one she was determined not to abandon just because that wretched man, Sylvester Jordan, wanted her to.

The following morning, Kat pulled on the same skirt and blouse for the third time in two days. She draped her sweater around her shoulders and told

16

her mother, 'I've got to go, Mum. Things to do, not least go home and change these clothes.'

'Are you busy this evening?' Ruth asked.

'Yes, I'm meeting Daisy. I had a booking yesterday morning for dinner for sixteen next Saturday. It's all a bit last-minute, so I urgently need to go over some things with her. Hopefully she'll be able to serve at table for me. I can't afford to let anything go wrong. Work's as rare as a blue moon at the moment.'

Ruth's expression took on a troubled aspect. Kat immediately felt guilty. Her mother was clearly nervous about being on her own overnight, but she really hadn't got the time to babysit her. She'd got too much preparation to do for Saturday. Once that was over, then things could change. For the bleak truth was, she had no further bookings.

'I'll call you afterwards, just to make sure everything's okay.'

'Oh, would you, darling? Thank you.'

17

'I must go. Bye.' Kat rushed from the shop and darted across the pavement, intending to cross the road to where her van was parked. She had already stepped off the pavement when she was startled by the screeching of tyres and the prolonged and loud blaring of a car horn. She leapt backwards, only just managing to stay upright, and then stared in outrage at the sight of a very expensive-looking red sports car, its long bonnet just inches from her. The next second the door was thrust open and a tall, powerfully built man climbed out. He immediately strode around the vehicle towards her, fury painted all over his good-looking face.

'Do you have a death wish, or did you have some other objective in mind?' he snapped sarcastically. 'Because if you want to die, you're going the right way about it.'

Kat looked at him, swallowed convulsively, and then closed her eyes, as if she could blot out the sight that was confronting her.

It was none other than Sylvester Jordan.

Of all the people for her to dart out in front of. She hadn't seen him in years, and she had to practically walk beneath his wheels. She opened her eyes again and stammered, 'N-no. Sorry, I wasn't looking.'

'Oh, really. Do you always walk into a busy road 'not looking'? Certainly a novel way of going about things.' His tone was one of pure sarcasm.

'I don't, no, and I've apologised.' *What more can I do?* she thought to herself. *Prostrate myself before you? Beg forgiveness?* She snorted softly. Not flippin' likely! Defiantly now, she lifted her head and returned his stare, just in time to see his eyes darkening and narrowing.

'Don't I know you?' he asked her.

She shrugged. 'I don't know. Do you?' Her heart began to race. Had he actually remembered her? In that second, she wasn't at all sure that she wanted him to.

'Yes, I do.' His gaze narrowed even further as he subjected her to intense scrutiny. 'You were at school the same time as me. You're — um — ' He began to look impatient now, critical even, as if his difficulty in recalling who she was could, in some convoluted way, be her fault.

She decided to put him out of his misery. 'Katrina Lucas. I go by Kat now, for short.' Immediately she regretted it. What the hell was she thinking? Had she no control over her tongue? Not only had she bumped — almost literally — into him, dressed in yesterday's crumpled clothes, with hair that was desperately in need of a good brushing, and not a scrap of make-up on her face; she also had to then go and blurt out her name. Why hadn't she simply stayed silent, and therefore anonymous? As it was, she couldn't have done any more if she'd intentionally tried to live up to his memories of her. Mind you, the way she was looking, it was a wonder he hadn't recognised her straight away.

He frowned at her now. 'Katrina? Oh yes, I remember. You were two years behind me at school.'

She didn't answer. She wasn't going to give him the satisfaction of knowing she'd recognised him instantly.

'Well, well. Yes, I recognise you now.' He tilted his head to one side, his stare a penetrating one.

She was tempted in that second to ask him if he also remembered the disparaging way he'd described her to his friend, but resisted. Instead, she decided to get a little of her own back. She frowned at him. 'And you are . . . ?'

Of course he saw straight through that. The amused and extremely knowing gleam in his eyes, and the quirk of his mouth, left her in no doubt. But all he said was, 'Sylvester Jordan. Jordan Enterprises. You've probably heard the name.'

'Oh,' she said, pretending surprise. 'I've certainly heard of it, yes. You're the company planning to evict my mother from her flower shop and build some sort of — um, now what is it?' She made great play of giving the question considerable thought before saying, 'Oh yes, department store.'

In the aftermath of that somewhat melodramatic performance, his expression darkened, as his jaw simultaneously exhibited all the properties of chiselled granite. 'Your mother?'

'Yes. She owns this shop.' She pointed over her shoulder to Petals. 'Tell me, I'm curious — did you have anything to do with the brick that was heaved through her window last night? You can see, if you take the time to look, the damage that was inflicted.'

His gaze moved beyond her to the window of Petals as he noticed the breakage, clearly for the first time. A single eyebrow lifted and the silver-grey of his eyes darkened dramatically before, just as she'd remembered from fifteen years ago, changing to the exact colour of wet slate. He swivelled his head and stared at her.

'Why the hell would I throw a brick through anyone's window?'

'Oh, I didn't mean you personally,' she exclaimed in honeyed tones. 'I meant one of your minions. I sure there must be people who'd be prepared to do such a thing for the right price.'

His features darkened even further, though she wouldn't have believed that possible. 'I'll ask you again — why would I, or anyone in my pay, want to throw a brick through someone's window?'

Kat made no attempt to hide her contempt. 'Oh, now let me see . . . She's refusing to move out, so . . . to frighten her? To force — oh, sorry — to *persuade* her to accept your offer to buy her out? After all, she's holding up all your plans, isn't she? The delay must be costing you money.'

He didn't utter a single word; he didn't have to. The expression in his eyes said it all, and was more than sufficient to make her tremble. 'I'll forget you said any of that,' he finally ground out. 'But just to make things crystal clear, I'm not, and never have been, in the business of terrifying women.'

'Well, as the late Mandy Rice-Davies might have said, you would say that, wouldn't you?' And then, before he could say anything else, she sang out, 'Well, things to do, places to go.' She wiggled her fingers in farewell before once more beginning to cross the road, this time taking inordinate and highly exaggerated care to make sure there wasn't an oncoming vehicle. She felt his gaze following her and grinned broadly to herself. First blood to her in the forthcoming battle, she rather thought. And in the light of that triumph, as small as it was, she had great difficulty in stopping herself from punching the air.

2

That evening, Kat met Daisy in the nearest pub to both of them, the Green Frog. Luckily, it was also their favourite pub: low-beamed ceilings, gently sloping wooden floors, blazing log fires in winter. The staff were friendly and it was never too crowded, because the majority of young people favoured the trendy wine bar further along the road.

Kat had spent the better part of the day trying to make up her mind about the menu for the following Saturday. In the end she had settled on two menus to show Daisy, hoping her friend would help her decide which one to select. Kat thought she might even go for some sort of combination of the two. As it was such short notice, Mrs Latimer had left the choice of food to Kat, but had asked Kat to email the menu to her for her approval. The only thing she'd stipulated was that it mustn't be 'the usual type of dinner party food, you know, chicken or salmon'.

The dinner was to be held on the twenty-fifth of October, which meant Kat had only a week to buy all the ingredients and then prepare as much of the food as she could in advance. It helped relieve the pressure on her on the day in question. Apparently it was Mr Latimer's fortieth birthday, and he'd expressly asked that his gift be something other than shirts, sweaters or cufflinks. Which had led to his wife opting for a dinner party; a dinner party that was to be a little different.

Such a rush was exactly what Kat hated. She liked time to plan properly; to carefully research where she could find the very best ingredients for the best price. And that was where the internet came in useful. But even that could take time, and time was what she didn't have. Such was her financial dilemma, however, that she couldn't afford to turn down any sort of lucrative work, last-minute or not. Though why anyone would leave the planning of such an important occasion to the last minute, she couldn't imagine.

Daisy looked at the two menus. 'Both of these look very time-consuming to prepare, as well as expensive.'

'I know, but the client wants something different, and she's willing to pay over the odds for it. I thought I could cook something from each menu. What do you think?' She glanced quizzically at her friend. 'Are you going to be free to help, both for the prep and the serving? I'll pay you a bit more.'

'Okay. Yeah, sure. I could use the money, actually. I'm a bit strapped at the moment. How many guests will there be?'

'Sixteen.' She eyed her friend then, slightly nervously. 'Um, you might not be so sure about helping when you hear what she wants us to wear.'

'Go on,' Daisy said, 'tell me the worst.'

'Well, it's to be a fancy-dress murder-mystery evening, and she wants us — '

'Different,' Daisy finished for her. 'How does that work then?'

'I've no idea. I'm just providing the food.'

'Right.'

'Um, she wants us — ' Again she eyed her friend. Would Daisy go along with what she was about to ask? They'd never done anything like it before.

'Go on,' Daisy impatiently urged. 'I'm imagining all sorts here. She doesn't want us to play corpses, does she?'

'No.' Kat took a deep breath and blurted, 'She wants us to dress as French maids.' There, she'd said it. 'She'll provide the costumes.'

'French maids?' Daisy cried. 'What? Short black dresses and frilly aprons?'

'I assume so, and she's paying enough that if she wanted us to dress up as clowns, I'd do it. I need this job, Daisy,' she could hear herself pleading.

'Business is terrible, you know that. I've nothing else booked after this one.'

'Yeah, the salon's a bit slow too. That's why I'm hard up; not many tips.' Daisy worked in a local hairdressing salon. The pay wasn't great, which was why she needed the extra that her tips provided and why she was glad of the work that Kat offered. If Kat's business folded, Daisy would also suffer. 'Of course I'll do it. Might be fun. Hey,' she added, her eyes glittering with curiosity, 'changing the subject, what's this I hear about your mum's shop being vandalised?'

'It happened last night. She's very upset, as well as being furious. Who told you about it? Oh, let me guess — the jungle drums have been active?'

'It was Mrs Baxter in the newsagent's.'

'That woman knows everything. I'm beginning to suspect she has some sort of inbuilt radar system as well a set of drums.'

'I think her customers keep her up to

date.' Daisy eyed Kat as if unsure whether to go on or not. 'Rumour is, Jordan Enterprises is behind it.'

Kat was horrified. What if Sylvester Jordan got wind of these rumours and assumed Kat was behind them? Which was quite likely after what she'd said to him. She had more or less accused him, if not of actually committing the crime, certainly of instigating it. Such a story was libellous, wasn't it? Or was it slanderous? She wasn't sure. She felt sick at the implications.

'Oh, good Lord, we don't know that. Who told Mrs Baxter?'

'She said it was Charlie Turnbull. He's been putting two and two together. It doesn't take much working out though, does it?'

Kat let out a sigh of relief. Sadly, that emotion didn't linger. Sylvester would still suspect the rumour had originated from her. Why hadn't she kept her big mouth shut? She was too impulsive by half, all too often speaking before her brain had engaged. It had landed her in trouble so many times. Why, she agonised, did she never learn?

She lifted her glass and took a hefty slug of red wine, only to choke on it when she saw who had just walked in. Only the man himself. And what was more, he was accompanied by another man who, from the look of him, could only be his assistant — partner? — Brett Sinclair. He certainly matched her mother's description.

Her heart raced, hammering painfully in her chest. Were they looking for her? Were they going to accuse her? *Oh, stop it*, she told herself. *Now you're being ridiculous.* They wouldn't have known she'd be here.

'Wow! Hello,' murmured Daisy. 'Talent alert at three o'clock.' She was staring at the two men, not bothering to hide her excited interest. 'Who are they? Do you know?'

'Well,' Kat managed to control her choking sufficiently to gasp, 'one's Sylvester Jordan; the other I assume is Brett Sinclair.' She had to admit they

31

made a striking pair: Sylvester, tall, dark-haired, handsome, with those fabulous silver-grey eyes; Brett — if it was indeed Brett — shorter and more heavily built, and attractive as well, with tawny blond hair and vivid blue eyes. She noticed the gaze of every woman in the pub turning towards them. A buzz of feverish speculation began. The two men, however, seemed utterly unaware of it.

But then, as if Sylvester sensed Kat's eyes upon him, he turned his head to look directly at her. His expression darkened with something that looked remarkably like irritation. She looked away, refusing to award him more than a second's attention. God forbid that he should think she was in any way interested in him. But — her heart once again lurched — what if he came over and demanded to know whether she was the one spreading malicious rumours about him? He'd never believe her denial, not after the way she'd spoken to him.

She took another hefty gulp of her wine. Dear Lord. If she wasn't careful, she was going to be adding to her already fairly large bundle of trouble by falling down drunk. She'd never been able to tolerate much in the way of alcohol. A single glass was more than enough to push her over the top of sobriety.

Daisy whispered, her mouth almost pressed to Kat's ear, 'They're coming over, and the dark one's mine!'

Jeez! She was welcome to him. Kat lifted her glass and took yet another substantial mouthful of wine. This one hit the spot, right where she needed it. On top of what she'd already gulped down, it imbued her with the courage to look up and meet Sylvester's slaty gaze.

'Hello again,' he said. 'I'd like to introduce you to Brett Sinclair. He works with me. Brett, this is Kat Lucas.' He paused before going on to ask, 'No after-effects from our near-collision this morning, I hope?'

She felt rather than saw Daisy turn her head to stare at her. 'You dark horse,' she muttered, just loudly enough for Kat to hear but no one else. 'You didn't say anything.'

Kat swivelled her head and glared at her friend before turning back to look up at Sylvester. She made an instantaneous decision. Didn't they say attack was always better than defence? Well, now was the perfect time to put that theory to the test. 'Fortunately, no,' she began. 'But I have to ask, do you always drive so quickly and so near to the kerb? Especially in built-up areas? I could have been a child, and who can say what would have happened then; what the consequences could have been?' Her manner was one of cool and calculated defiance. There was no indication of the sick apprehension she'd felt just seconds ago at seeing him walk in. She felt proud of herself. Maybe she should gulp back the wine more often.

'I was keeping rigorously to the speed

limit — as I always do,' he replied. 'You should take a good look both ways before blindly stepping into the road. Weren't you taught the Green Cross Code? It would seem your education was sadly lacking.'

'I did look,' she retorted. 'Just because you drive an expensive car, it doesn't give you licence to disregard other road users.'

But her argument was a weak one. She knew she hadn't looked; Sylvester knew she hadn't looked. Even so, he didn't respond this time. Instead, he tilted his head to one side and from beneath heavy eyelids lazily examined as much of her as he could see. She might as well have been naked, so penetrating was his scrutiny. She felt her face flame. She so rarely blushed nowadays, and that he should be the one to provoke it made her want to scream with vexation.

She heard Brett say, 'Come on, I see some free seats over there.' Sylvester ignored him; he was still looking at Kat.

She boldly returned his stare. Her breathing quickened, and she could have sworn his breathing had too. But that was ridiculous, wasn't it? He couldn't be as affected by her as she seemed to be by him. Yet, there was something in his gaze; a hot smouldering that suggested he wasn't entirely immune to her.

'Vester,' Brett said, 'let's go before someone else nabs them.'

For a moment more, it was if Sylvester just hadn't heard Brett; but then, still not removing his gaze from Kat, he said, 'Okay. Well, have a good evening, Kat. I have to say, you've changed dramatically from our school-days.'

'I should hope so,' Kat retaliated. 'It was a long time ago.' Then, daringly, she went on to ask, 'For better or worse?'

'Well, let's just say it's a wonder I recognised you.'

He had neatly avoided answering her question. About to leave, he suddenly seemed to become aware of Daisy's presence. 'I'm sorry,' he said, looking at her, 'we haven't been introduced.'

Daisy preened. 'I'm Daisy.' To Kat's horror, she actually fluttered her eyelashes. God knew what Sylvester would make of that. She waited with bated breath for the inevitable put-down, the sarcastic remark. 'You wouldn't have known me at school.'

But Kat's fears proved groundless. His reply, when it came, was polite and gallant. 'I'm very pleased to meet you, Daisy. Maybe I'll see you around sometime.'

Daisy actually wriggled in her seat as she throatily murmured, 'I do hope so.'

Kat watched as Sylvester smiled appreciatively down at her. 'Well, I'll be seeing you then — both of you, I'm sure.'

The second the two men had gone, Daisy said, 'So come on, tell all. What happened this morning?'

Kat softly related the sequence of events. She didn't want her words reaching Sylvester, and she'd noticed his slanting glances their way. Whether directed at her or Daisy she couldn't have said. He'd seemed to like what he saw when he was speaking to her friend. Strangely, that inspired a feeling of disappointment. Impatiently, she shrugged it off. She really didn't care who he was attracted to.

'My God,' Daisy breathed, 'I'd have fallen at his feet simply to get him to pick me up. I've heard all about him, of course.'

'Of course you have,' Kat ironically put in. 'Being one of the most frequent visitors to the newsagent's.'

Daisy ignored that and went on, 'I can't believe you actually accused him of heaving a brick through your mum's shop window. Wow!'

'Well, not in so many words . . . ' But she had done exactly that.

'So do you know how long he's been back?'

Kat found herself glancing over at Sylvester. Maddeningly, his smile back at her was only a fraction short of smug. He knew they were talking about him. Kat gnawed at her bottom lip. And that just demonstrated how arrogant he was. So arrogant, he probably thought himself the centre of the universe and that the rest of the world revolved around him. Still, she was truly thankful that the rumours and speculation about his part in the vandalism of Petals didn't seem to have reached his ears. She half-turned so that her back was to him. She wouldn't be surprised if he could lip-read, as he seemed able to do practically everything else. In any case, she was taking no chances, no chances at all. She'd already riled him enough for one day.

'I'm not exactly sure. It's fairly recently. You'll have to ask Mrs Baxter. She'll know for certain.'

'Well, it's long enough to have bought that huge house outside of town. Must have set him back a few million,' Daisy gushed. 'He's got it all, hasn't he? Good looks, sex appeal by the bucketful, and shedloads of money to boot.' She sighed. 'Do you think he liked me?'

'Good heavens, how should I know?'

'I think he does. That smile . . . ' She sighed rapturously. 'He's got two small boys, you know.'

'Yes, I know. I read a piece about him not long ago.'

'Divorced too, so single and available.' She licked her lips provocatively, at the same time gazing over Kat's shoulder towards Sylvester. She couldn't have made her interest plainer.

Kat resisted the temptation to look as well. She wasn't going to give him anything else to feel smug about. Daisy was doing more than enough of that as it was. 'Is there anything you don't know?' she bit out.

'Not much, no. You should visit Mrs Baxter. You'd get all the local news then, too.'

'News?' Kat scornfully asked. 'Don't you mean the local gossip?'

'So you aren't interested then?'

Kat remained tellingly silent.

'Exactly,' Daisy pronounced with a smile of irritating self-satisfaction.

If Kat hadn't known better, she'd have sworn her friend had been taking lessons from Sylvester Jordan. Actually, now that Kat came to consider the matter, Sylvester and Daisy would make a perfect match. They could have regular contests, seeing which one could outdo the other in the smugness stakes. But she was pretty sure Sylvester would win outright if it came to it.

'Listen up. There's more,' Daisy said.

Kat winced. She fervently hoped Sylvester couldn't hear any of this. She couldn't help herself then; she glanced back at him. As if he sensed her interest, he swivelled his head and held her gaze, once more inspiring a fiery blush.

She ground her teeth together. She'd long since grown out of such a girlish tendency, so why was she succumbing to it now? Must be his good looks. She snorted. Not that she was going to allow herself to be swayed by them. She'd had her fill of good-looking men. She'd been married to one, after all, and look how that had turned out. With the worst kind of betrayal.

She'd only known Max six months when he proposed. She always said he'd swept her off her feet, literally. He was striding in that self-assured way he had, around a corner. Kat had been rushing towards him. Before she could do anything to avoid him, they'd collided, and Max had managed to catch her before she fell, lifting her off her feet to stare into her eyes and murmur, 'Bella, bella.' She should have realised then he was a ladies' man. But she hadn't, and very quickly she fell in love. He proposed and they were married within four months, when Kat was just twenty-one. It had been a small ceremony, neither of them wishing for a fuss. No wonder, she told herself later on. For his part, he hadn't wanted his married lover finding out.

He carried on his double life for the

next three years before Kat finally discovered the truth behind all his 'travelling for business'. She relentlessly berated herself for her complete stupidity and, not knowing what else to do, she'd stalked out of the marital home, unable to bear living with such a complete rat any longer, and returned to her parents' house. When that didn't work out — Ruth had developed a very bossy streak, attempting to dominate her daughter as well as her long-suffering husband — Kat found herself a flat to rent and, going out on a limb, managed to secure a bank loan and started her catering business. Luckily there were no children, so there was no one but her to grieve over what had happened.

Ruth's first words when Kat told her what Max had been up to had been: 'I never liked him. Neither did your father.' But she'd found herself wondering afterwards if her marriage breakdown had been what had contributed to her father's fatal heart attack.

It had happened just six months later.

Thankfully, Max had moved away once the decree absolute was granted, and she hadn't heard from him since. And that suited her. She had no wish to see him ever again. She'd even reverted to her maiden name. She'd wanted nothing to remind her of her disastrous marriage.

And with these thoughts, her determination not to be taken in by another handsome man hardened. Not one of them could be trusted; certainly not the unscrupulous Sylvester Jordan. She'd as soon trust a rattlesnake. She turned back to Daisy and said, 'Sorry, what were you saying?'

'Just that his two boys are only small; two and three and a half years old, I believe. And, unusually, he's managed to get full custody. Must be because their mother ran off with another man not long after the youngest was born. In fact, the way I heard it, he might not even be Sylvester's son . . . ' Daisy's words trailed off. 'Earth to Kat, earth to

Kat. Come in, Kat. Are you even listening?'

'Of course,' Kat indignantly said.

'Well, you could have fooled me. Mind you, if you didn't keep staring over your shoulder at a certain person . . . '

'I'm not.' Kat spoke even more indignantly now.

'So what were you looking at then? The pattern of the wallpaper?'

'Oh, shut up. Let's get back to the menus, shall we?'

'Gladly. That's what we're here for, after all.'

* * *

Saturday came round all too quickly and Kat drove to her client's house, her small van packed with everything she'd need for the preparation of the evening's meal. Daisy was coming a little later, after the salon closed at four o'clock. She mainly waited at table on her own, but with sixteen people sitting down it would need both of them, so Kat needed to get ahead with the preparation of the food. She had prepared as much as she could beforehand, but there was still a considerable amount to be done. Daisy could help with that when she arrived, as they'd agreed.

It was quite a complicated menu, starting with French onion soup with cognac and goat's cheese croutons, followed by crab and prawn cakes garnished with a watercress sauce and a rocket salad. The main course was beef Wellington, which Kat didn't consider particularly different, but Mrs Latimer had been adamant that was what she wanted once she'd turned down Kat's suggestion of rack of lamb. 'And don't try and get away with cheap steak. It must be fillet,' she had stipulated. This was to be accompanied by tiny new potatoes, buttered carrots, asparagus spears wrapped in bacon, and fresh green peas. There would then be a lemon sorbet followed by a choice of raspberry pavlova or a tarte tatin with Chantilly cream. The meal would end with an extensive cheese board, coffee, and petit fours which Kat had, of course, made herself.

By the time Daisy arrived, Kat was more or less at the stage she'd planned to be, but there were several last-minute tasks to be completed with regards to the food preparation, and the table still wasn't laid in the dining room. The hostess had asked for that to be done and also decorated with seasonal foliage and flowers.

Daisy immediately set about that task. She was the artistic half of the duo. Plus she was responsible for uncorking the wines to allow them to 'breathe'. The hostess had nothing to do other than make sure her husband had a good day, and then get herself ready for the evening. That didn't prevent her from indulging in frequent excursions to the kitchen, where she managed to hinder Kat and Daisy in every possible way. Somehow, though,

Kat managed to hold her tongue. She was making a hefty profit on the evening, so a little irritation had to be borne.

Finally, by six thirty everything was ready. Kat and Daisy went upstairs to put on their French maid costumes. A bedroom had been put at their disposal, and the outfits would be hanging on the outside of a large wardrobe.

Daisy went into the room first and stared at the garments. She then let her breath out in a long, slow whistle. 'Ohmygod,' she breathed. Then, more slowly, 'Oh. My. God.'

3

Kat, quickly following her friend into the room, also stared, aghast, at the sight that confronted her. Even suspended on hangers, she could see how much bare flesh the outfits would expose. The dresses were black and figure-hugging, with plunging necklines and flared skirts that would almost certainly finish halfway up their thighs. There were two pairs of very high-heeled black shoes along with a couple of pairs of sheer black hold-up stockings. Frilly white aprons hung from the waists of the dresses to a couple of inches above the hems of the full skirts. There were also two frilly caps for their heads.

'I refuse to wear that,' Daisy burst out after a stunned silence. 'We'll be half-naked.'

Kat could see only too well what

Daisy meant. But if they refused to wear the outfits, Mrs Latimer might refuse to pay, and frankly Kat couldn't afford to risk that. She was relying on the profit from the evening's work to help with her gas and electricity bills. Then there was her community tax which would soon be due, as well as a much-needed service for her van. And on top of all of that, the vehicle would soon need a set of new tyres. All of which didn't leave much — much? — It didn't leave anything for her day-to-day living expenses. She sighed. It was hopeless. She needed more work, and soon, otherwise . . .

'Let's put them on,' she tentatively suggested. 'They might look better then.'

Daisy snorted her incredulity, but she did as Kat suggested. Being a good three inches shorter than Kat's five feet six and nowhere near as voluptuous, Daisy actually looked okay. The dress was longer and very little cleavage was on display. Not that she had much to reveal anyway, as she repeatedly bemoaned. Kat, however . . .

'Oh my God,' Daisy once again said. 'You'll give every man in the room a heart attack.'

Kat regarded herself in the mirror and gasped in dismay. Her breasts bulged above the neckline, her cleavage deep and alluring. As for the skirt, it finished a good eight inches above her knees. She tried tugging it down, tugging the tight bodice up; nothing worked. The greater part of her was still on display; embarrassingly so. As she always did when anxious or distressed, she chewed at her bottom lip. The dress was sending out all the wrong signals. And how were they supposed to walk around in such high heels all evening, and serving food to boot? There was one good thing, at least: the tops of the stockings reached up beyond the hemline of the dress — just, so no bare flesh was exposed there; not at the moment, at any rate. But then, she wasn't moving either.

She groaned. All she needed was a pole to dance around and the picture would be complete. 'I'll go and see Mrs Latimer,' she said. 'I can't wear this; I simply can't.'

'You have to,' Daisy urged, executing a complete and exasperating U-turn. 'You agreed — and she's paying megabucks, isn't she? Anyway, everyone's going to be in fancy dress, aren't they?'

Kat nodded. She was way beyond words by this stage. She couldn't take her eyes away from the image reflected in the full-length mirror.

'So there's bound to be other women dressed in similar fashion,' Daisy added.

'What? As French maids? I doubt it.'

'No, I meant with plunging necklines. Anyway, there won't be anyone present who'll know you; so really, who cares?'

'Says the woman who's decently covered,' Kat tightly riposted.

Daisy ignored that. 'So if no one

knows you, does it matter if you're showing . . . well, a bit more than you usually do?'

'A bit more?' Kat cried. 'It'll be a great deal more than a bit every time I bend over to serve someone,' she miserably wailed. 'You're right, I look half-naked.'

Daisy eyed her. 'You look rather gorgeous, actually. Very sexy. I'd give everything I own to look like you do.'

'Would you?' Kat eyed her own reflection doubtfully now. 'Really?'

'Yeah. Go on, do it. It might be fun, and it will give the birthday boy a bit of a treat. He won't have been expecting this sort of gift, I don't suppose. Not in a million years.'

Kat still looked very doubtful, despite her friend's encouraging remarks. 'Supposing his wife doesn't like it?'

'Well, she shouldn't have supplied such skimpy costumes then, should she?' Daisy bluntly said.

Kat couldn't argue with that. However, it very swiftly proved anything but fun — for Kat, at least.

Because the second she walked into the dining room to begin serving the soup, the first person she saw was Sylvester Jordan. He was also the first to spot her, and his gaze transformed into one of unabashed and unmistakable lust; this was immediately followed by gasps from all of the other men present. One man even went so far as to say, 'Can I have her for the first course? Forget the soup.' Only to receive a sharp jab in the ribs from the woman at his side; his wife, presumably.

As for Kat, she just wanted the ground beneath her to open up and swallow her. Especially when she glanced back at Sylvester and noted the gleam that still illuminated his eyes. He was enjoying this — positively glorying in her embarrassment, in fact. The beast.

And with that, she suspected her ordeal was only just beginning.

She wasn't wrong.

Sylvester's now narrowed but piercing stare followed her progress round the table. A fleeting glance down told her why. Just as she'd feared, every time she leaned forward she exposed another couple of inches of shadowy cleavage. And that wasn't all. She must also be displaying an equal amount of thigh as her skirt rose behind her.

When she finally got to him, he murmured, 'So nice to see you again — and so much more of you.' After which, he grinned up at her.

Her fingers itched to slap him. Either that, or drop the hot contents of her tureen onto his lap. However, she limited herself to a tight-lipped, 'It's not my choice of costume, I can assure you.' Then, as she appraised his plain jacket, shirt and trousers, she couldn't resist asking, 'Who are you meant to be?'

'I couldn't think of anything, so I came as myself. I'm not really into fancy dress.'

'How very unimaginative of you,

when everyone else has made so much of an effort.' She glanced around at all the other guests. Snow White was there, as was Prince Charming. Henry VIII was present with a woman who she guessed was intended to be Anne Boleyn. A pirate was accompanied by his buxom lady who, to Kat's relief, was exposing even more cleavage than she was. In fact, if the neckline were any lower, she'd be exposing her navel. 'Maybe you should have considered Attila the Hun, or even Vlad the Impaler.'

She moved on then to the next guest, ignoring his snort of something that could have been mirth but was much more likely to have been derision. He was probably accustomed to being waited on by demure and subservient women; women who would do exactly as they were told without talking back. Well, that definitely wasn't her. Whatever he decided to throw at her, she'd return with gusto.

From then on, she made a point of

avoiding his eye. Though she did note the also conventionally dressed woman at his side — his girlfriend? — shooting venomous stares her way, even muttering to her hostess at one point: 'Really, Grace, where did you find her? The local brothel?'

Throughout it all, Kat remained agonisingly conscious of Sylvester and his frequent glances. In the end she defiantly returned his stare, only to watch as his eyes roamed lazily over her, ultimately provoking the dreaded blush which she seemed disturbingly prone to whenever she found herself in his company.

Finally, as she was placing the cheese board on the table, he beckoned her over and said, 'I do quite a lot of entertaining. Could you let me have a business card?' She saw that infuriating gleam illuminating his eyes again as he asked, 'And tell me, what other costumes do you have?'

'None,' she snapped. 'Your hostess provided this one. It's not something I usually agree to.'

'Oh, what a shame. I can think of several getups I'd like to see you in.'

Outraged, she glared back at him, only to have to watch as amusement flirted with the corners of his mouth. Again, she was sorely tempted to drop something on him — the complete cheese board, maybe? Or better still, the remains of the tarte tatin. She visualised what was left of the syrupy fruit dripping from his head. It was her turn now to glint with amusement.

As soon as the meal was over and coffee had been served, the guests embarked on their murder mystery game, accompanied by a great deal of hilarity and plenty of shrieking. After changing out of their French maids' garb, Kat and Daisy retired to the kitchen and made a start on the clearing up. This took some time, even with a dishwasher. Eventually Kat said to Daisy, 'You might as well go. I can finish up.'

Daisy didn't argue. She was looking

tired. Kat was just finishing packing back into their boxes the items of equipment she always made a point of taking with her, when Sylvester strode into the kitchen.

'Good, I've caught you. I've come for one of your cards. Did you forget?' he guilelessly asked, his expression informing her that he was well aware that she'd deliberately disregarded his request. 'I meant what I said. I entertain on a fairly regular basis, and although my housekeeper is quite satisfactory for plain cooking, I do need something a bit more elaborate than shepherd's pie on those occasions.'

Kat had been hoping he'd have forgotten asking for her card — even though she was desperate for work. 'Oh — well . . . ' she began.

'I promise I won't make you wear anything you don't want to. Though I have to admit this evening's outfit was particularly fetching.' He grinned teasingly at her. 'This one is — ' He lowered his gaze to the jeans and shirt that she was once more wearing. ' — less fetching.' His smiling features rearranged themselves into an expression of mock disapproval.

Kat almost smiled — almost — as she opened her handbag to bring out one of the cards she always carried with her. She waved it at him.

'Thank you.' He studied it intently. 'Katering For U. Clever. A play on your name, I presume?' She nodded. 'I also presume it's your own business?'

'Of course.'

He cocked his head at her and asked, 'How's it going at the moment?' He did seem genuinely interested. Even so, she was guarded in her reply. She wasn't about to admit she was struggling to find work.

'Fine. Yes — good.'

'So what dates do you have free?'

'What dates are you thinking of?' Why on earth had she blurted that out? Now he'd be bound to put two and two together and come up with the sobering fact that she hadn't got anything else booked at present. Nonetheless, she reached for her handbag and dragged her diary out. She couldn't afford to turn anything down, even if the customer was the detestable Sylvester Jordan.

'Can I ring you?' he said. 'I don't have my diary with me. At a guess, I'd say a fortnight from today, but I'll confirm that. Would you be available then?'

Turning away from him, she made a play of checking that date, knowing full well it was available. 'Yes, that would be okay.' She spoke grudgingly as she swung to face him again. The last person she wanted to do anything for was him, the man she suspected of trying to force her mother from her home.

He proceeded to study her, his expression a knowing one. Surely he hadn't read her thoughts. 'Right. I'll be in touch then.' He paused, and then went on, 'The food was perfect, by the way. You're a very talented cook.'

'Thank you.' A surge of pleasure suffused her at his compliment, so much so that she somehow dredged up a smile. He smiled back; and it was then that something strange and quite unexpected happened. She experienced a powerful and unmistakable jolt of desire.

'Goodnight then,' he said. 'I'll ring you.'

* * *

True to his word, Sylvester rang the next morning. He didn't waste any time on polite preliminaries, but got straight to the point. 'The Saturday I mentioned last night is good for me,' he said, and gave her the date.

'Okay,' Kat replied, 'I'll book you in for then.'

'I wondered ... ' He paused, astonishingly sounding a bit unsure of himself. ' ... if we could meet this evening and discuss the menu?'

'Oh, sorry. I already have a date.' She gnawed at her lip. She'd made it sound as if she were regarding their meeting as a date instead of a business meeting. 'I mean an engagement — well, that is to say — it is a date. I didn't mean yours and my meeting would be a date . . . ' She let her words trail off. She was just making the whole thing worse with her ineffectual protests.

'It's okay, Kat.' She could tell by his tone that he was grinning. She ground her teeth together. Why did he seem to have this effect on her? She was usually perfectly composed. 'I understood what you meant.'

'I-I can do tomorrow at a time to suit you,' she went on, struggling to be business-like and competent instead of the adolescent she'd just sounded like.

'Good.' And he did sound genuinely pleased. 'So, shall we say seven o'clock in the Green Frog? And, Kat, just so you don't mistake it for a date, could you bring a selection of your menus with you?'

This time she didn't simply grind her teeth together, she positively gnashed them. He seemed to take an inordinate amount of pleasure in winding her up. Not that she was going to let him know that he succeeded — every time. So she coolly responded, 'Certainly, I fully intended to. There couldn't be any other reason for us to meet, could there?'

'Perhaps not this time, but who knows what the future holds? I wouldn't rule anything out.' And he rang off.

Kat stared at the phone, a frown tugging at her brow. What the hell did that mean? That he intended to ask her out on a date sometime in the future? Well, he needn't waste his time, because the moon would have to have turned to cream cheese before she'd agree to that.

* * *

That evening Kat met Ben, the man she was currently seeing. They'd been meeting on a regular basis for three months now. That didn't mean they were a couple; at least, not in Kat's view. She liked Ben; in fact she'd known him since their schooldays. But he was just a friend. However, she'd had the suspicion of late that he was starting to want more, and that made her doubt the wisdom of continuing to meet him.

She enjoyed his company; he made her laugh with his pronounced sense of the ridiculous. But he didn't . . . well, excite her, she supposed was the right word. His kiss was pleasant, but that was all it was. Her heart didn't miss a beat when she saw him; her pulse didn't race. Her body didn't flame with passion or desire.

She frowned. It wasn't just Ben that she couldn't seem to respond to. It was every man she'd dated for the past five years. Could it be that she'd grown frigid; incapable of loving someone, of wanting someone? Had Max ruined any chance of that for her? Any chance of trusting a man again? She sighed.

So it was all the more disturbing to admit that Sylvester's glances, albeit teasingly provocative, had somehow achieved those things with little or no effort.

Ben was already waiting for her when she arrived at the pub, as was her customary glass of wine. He was like an eager puppy. If he possessed a tail, it would be frantically wagging. Maybe she should tell him how she felt and put an end to his hopes; that would be the fair thing to do.

He waved to her and smiled. All Kat felt was a lowering of her spirits. She walked towards him — and as she did so, she became aware of someone watching her. She glanced around and saw Sylvester. God, he was like the proverbial bad penny, turning up when least expected or wanted. He was standing at the bar alone, and yes, he was watching her from beneath heavy lids. How had he known she'd be here this evening? Because she was as sure as she could be that that was the reason he was standing there.

She felt her heartbeat quicken, and her pulses began to throb, reverberating right through her. Even her face felt hot. How was it that he could do this to her with one look, when Ben — who did everything right, everything he could to try and please her — couldn't?

Sylvester inclined his head to her; she did exactly the same, and walked straight on past.

'Hi,' Ben said as she approached their table. 'Who's that?' He nodded toward Sylvester.

'Sylvester Jordan,' she told him. 'Don't you remember him? We were all at school at the same time.'

'God, yes. Is that him? I heard he was back. I didn't recognise him.'

Kat slanted a fleeting glance towards Sylvester and then quickly looked away again. He was still watching them. Again, she felt the warmth spread over her face. She just hoped Ben didn't notice.

'I also heard he's done extremely well for himself.'

'He has, yes. He's asked me to cater a dinner party for him.'

Ben looked surprised. 'Isn't he married? Surely his wife would do that.'

'He's divorced. I'm meeting him here — tomorrow evening, actually — to discuss the menu.'

Ben's expression darkened at that. 'How come his girlfriend isn't cooking for him and his cronies? Come to think of it, looking at her, she doesn't seem the sort to toil in the kitchen.' He snorted contemptuously.

'His girlfriend?' Kat couldn't stop herself. She glanced back to where she'd last seen Sylvester standing. He wasn't there. A quick glance round the room located him, sitting at a table with the glamorous woman who'd been at his side at the Latimers' dinner party. So they were a couple, and he wasn't here simply to see Kat. Well good, that was good. The trouble was it didn't feel that way, not in the slightest. She

68

frowned. Why the hell was she bothered about what Sylvester Jordan was doing?

She turned back to Ben, but not before rearranging her expression into one of complete unconcern. 'He was with her last night.'

'Hah! He's probably got her lined up as wife number two then. His sort seem to jump from one wife to the next pretty damn smartly. What is it they call them? Trophy wives — yeah, that's it.' He snorted again. 'I seem to remember all the girls at school swooning over him.'

'Don't include me in that statement,' Kat waspishly said. She'd always hoped she'd hidden her own crush on Sylvester.

'Well, I do recall wondering if you had a bit of a thing for him.' He eyed her across the top of his glass as he took a hefty swig of beer.

'Very fleetingly, I can assure you. I quickly realised the sort of boy he was.'

'Oh.' He raised an eyebrow at her. 'And what sort was that?'

'The sort you've just described. A shallow flirt. I'm sure he hasn't changed.'

'You'd better watch yourself then.'

Kat stared quizzically at him. He couldn't have noticed her responses to Sylvester, could he?

'If you're going to be visiting his house and cooking for him.'

A pang of relief made itself felt. 'You needn't worry about that. I can take good care of myself. I'm not that impressionable teenager anymore.'

'No, you're not, are you?' he enigmatically said. 'I'm as sure as hell not making any impression on you.'

Kat chose not to answer that, and the evening progressed along its customary lines — until they were walking home, that was: Kat to her nearby flat and Ben to his rented house a bit further along the same road.

Out of the blue, he asked, 'Are we going anywhere in this relationship, Kat? To me it doesn't feel as if we are. In fact, what we have can barely be described as a relationship at all.'

Here it was, the moment Kat had been expecting. She should have pre-empted it and spoken out herself. The only reason she hadn't was that she had no wish to hurt Ben. But he was right to ask the question, and she owed him the truth. It was up to him whether they continued the way they were or ended things.

'I like you, Ben, I do. I enjoy your company. You make me laugh.'

'I don't make your pulses race though, do I? Or your heart beat faster.'

'Well, no,' she reluctantly conceded, 'but I value your friendship.'

'I want more than that, Kat.'

'I don't think I can give you more, Ben. Whether that will change in the future . . . ' She shrugged.

'I know Max hurt you deeply, but you can't allow him to wreck the rest of your life. You're a young, lovely woman. You deserve happiness with a man you love.' He swung to face her and put both hands on her shoulders. 'Let's try a little experiment, shall we?'

'Uh, what exactly? I'm not really into — '

'Stop talking,' he murmured, pulling her to him and kissing her. Not the gentle, almost platonic kiss he'd given her on previous occasions, but a kiss that was full of passion, his mouth grinding over hers, forcing her lips apart before plunging his tongue deep within. Kat tried to respond, but it was no good. She felt nothing, other than a disturbing sensation of revulsion.

He lifted his mouth from hers but kept his arms around her for a moment before rather roughly pushing her away. 'Kat, please — I've fallen for you, big time. Give us a chance. Try a bit harder.' He pulled her to him again, bending his head to hers once more. This time his kiss was an angry one, brutal even, as if he were punishing her. She made no move to free herself, frightened of inflaming his passions even further. Instead, she stood quite still within the circle of his arms until he, at last and reluctantly, released her.

'I'm sorry, Ben.'

He stared at her, his face full of misery, his eyes shiny with moisture. 'I know you are. I think it's time to call it quits, don't you? We both deserve better. More.' Kat nodded.

He kissed her again, gently, and this time she did muster up a response. Not the sort he wanted, she was sure, but it was a response — which was why she failed to see the red sports car driving slowly by, allowing the driver — as well as his attractive companion — time to see what was going on. Once he had, he put his foot down hard on the accelerator and disappeared round the next bend in the road.

Not long afterwards, Ben and Kat parted and Kat returned to her flat, feeling unaccountably depressed and lonely.

She'd been home for a couple of hours when her mobile phone rang. It was her mother.

'You'll never guess what he's done

now. He's only gone and pushed a load of filth through the shop letterbox. It looks, and smells, like horse manure.' Her voice broke. 'Come round — please? I'm scared, really scared. What if he decides to break in next time and — and physically threaten me?'

4

'I'm sure whoever it is won't do that.'

'Are you?' Ruth snapped. 'I wish I was.'

'Okay, I'll be with you in ten minutes. And if you haven't already, call the police.' Though what they could do, Kat didn't really know — unless they actually caught the culprit in the act, of course.

Ruth was near-hysterical by the time she arrived. Paul, the police constable who'd attended last time, was there, alone on this occasion. Had the powers that be decided not to waste the time of two men on what must look like a pretty hopeless case?

He regarded both women, his sympathy plain to see. 'There's not a lot we can do, Mrs Lucas. Did you catch any sign of the perpetrator? Anything at all? The smallest clue?'

'No, I didn't even hear him. It was the smell drifting up the stairs as I went to bed that alerted me. I don't know how long before that it was done.'

'Hmmm, that's a pity. The only thing I can recommend is that you stay alert, and if you see anyone — or anything — that worries you, ring us immediately. Don't, whatever you do, tackle him on your own.'

'Oh, don't worry. I'm not that brave. Or stupid.'

Once he'd gone, Kat indicated her hurriedly packed overnight bag and said, 'I'll stay if you like, just for a couple of nights.'

'Oh, darling, would you? That would be wonderful.'

'I've got to go out tomorrow evening to meet — ' She paused. Maybe now wasn't the best time to mention the fact that she was meeting Sylvester. She'd wait till Ruth had calmed down a little. ' — a client.'

'Oh, anyone I know?'

'No.' Which wasn't a lie, not in the

strictest sense of the word. Ruth didn't actually know him; she knew all about him but had never met him.

Once they'd cleared away the mess and wrapped it securely in several layers of newspaper and dropped it into the dustbin, they once more made up the bed in the tiny spare room.

'Will you be okay in here again?' Ruth asked, glancing anxiously around. 'You could have my bed.'

'And where would you sleep?'

'Well, in here, obviously.'

'No need, Mum. It's only for a couple of nights. Just till you get over your nervousness.'

'Huh! That's not going to happen anytime soon. Not until they catch him.'

Kat studied her mother's pale face. She looked deeply troubled; so much so, there were stark shadows underscoring her eyes. She was clearly frightened. 'Look, if you like I'll stay for a while longer. Perhaps if there's two of us, we'll manage to see who it is and catch them in the act if we're lucky.'

The relief on Ruth's face was instantaneous. 'Are you sure? What about your catering work?'

'I cook almost everything in the client's kitchen, and I can return to my flat during the day if I need to. I've got nothing booked for the next fortnight anyway.'

Again, she decided not to mention Sylvester's booking. There was time enough for that nearer to the date.

★　★　★

Kat's sleep that night was punctuated by disturbing dreams of intruders trying to gain entry to the shop and the flat above, and they all had Sylvester's good-looking features. When she finally peered at her wristwatch and saw that it was four o'clock, she gave up trying to sleep and got up. There was no sound from her mother's room, so she quietly made herself a pot of tea.

She'd have to go back to her flat

first thing to collect more clothes and fetch her catalogue of menus to show Sylvester that evening. But that wouldn't take long. She decided to use the free time to try and drum up some business, because the way she was going, she'd soon need to find some full-time paid employment. The bills were starting to come in again and she was once again struggling to find the funds to pay them. The profit she'd made on the Latimers' dinner had already disappeared and she was back to exactly where she'd been before, with no spare cash. She decided she'd place an advert in each of the local papers and see what that brought in.

* * *

By seven o'clock that evening, she was ready to go and meet Sylvester at the Green Frog. Even though she was back at Ruth's, the pub was still within walking distance, so she left her van parked outside Petals.

She didn't dress up for the meeting, other than to swap her jeans and shirt for a slim-line knee-length skirt, opaque black tights, and a lightweight sweater. For the past couple of days they'd been enjoying a brief Indian summer, which meant the evenings were relatively warm. It also meant people still weren't having formal dinner parties.

She walked into the lounge bar of the pub and spotted Sylvester in the far corner. He'd managed to secure a relatively secluded table for them. He saw her and immediately got to his feet.

'I was a bit early,' he said with a smile, 'so I've already got a beer. What can I get you?'

'Red wine, please.'

Once they were settled with their respective drinks, Kat opened her large bag and dragged out her catalogue of menus, followed by a thick notepad, a couple of pens, her diary and her phone, all of which she laid out one by one and side by side on the table before her.

'You've come well prepared, I see.'

A quizzical eyebrow lifted, whether in amusement or impatience with her exactitude she couldn't have said. Or maybe he suspected she was simply buying herself some time. For the fact was, she wasn't looking forward to what would be a business discussion with Sylvester Jordan. He must be accustomed to dealing with pre-eminent and highly professional people and, in the process, more than holding his own. The most she could hope for was to not make too big a fool of herself.

'There wouldn't be much point in turning up unprepared, would there?' she curtly replied. 'There are fifteen different menus in all, ranging in price and complete with photographs; but if there's anything you'd like that's not on them, I'm sure I'll be able to accommodate you.'

'I'm sure you will,' he softly murmured.

She glanced sharply at him. The innuendo would have been difficult to miss. She thrust the catalogue at him, then watched as he leafed through the pages. He reached the last page, which detailed the most expensive menu, and said, 'This one looks perfect.'

'It's seven courses, if you count the coffee and petit fours,' she remarked.

'Yes. Is there a problem with that?' Again he raised an eyebrow at her, and again she felt as if she were being judged and found far short of his expectations.

'No, not at all.' But the truth was, it was a menu that she'd only prepared once, and it entailed a lot of work. It consisted of individual asparagus and broccoli mini-quiches on a bed of rocket and watercress leaves, sole Veronique, fillet steak Diane with sautéed potatoes and the client's choice of four types of vegetables, and a lemon sorbet, then a choice between crêpes Suzette, fresh fruit salad in a white rum jus, and sticky toffee pudding, followed by a selection of French and English cheeses. It ended with coffee and petit fours.

'That's fine,' Kat added. She just hoped that Daisy would be able to give her a hand. She could, of course, prepare some of it beforehand in her own kitchen. 'How many guests will there be?'

'Twelve, probably. I'll have to confirm that with you.'

She found herself wondering if the glamorous blonde would be one of them. Though why she should care, she didn't know. 'What time would you want to sit down?'

'We'll aim for eight o'clock. Again, I'll confirm that.'

She began to make notes. 'Will you supply the wines, or do you want me to do that?' she asked, every inch the professional — she hoped.

'No, I'll take care of that myself. All I want from you is . . . ' He paused, and Kat found herself wondering what was coming next. If he said the wearing of a French maid's costume, he could go whistle. However, all he said was,

' . . . the food. Oh, and the service, of course.' He then gave her an enigmatic smile. She couldn't believe it: he'd known what she was thinking. He had to be the most maddening man she'd ever encountered. Also the most shrewd.

'Of course. That's covered in the cost.'

'Good. So tell me — ' He leaned back in his seat, his posture one of total relaxation. ' — where did you undertake your training to become such an excellent chef?'

'I didn't have any formal training as such. I did attend a couple of courses — one in French cuisine, the other a pastry and dessert course. Other than that, I'm self-taught. I helped my mother from the age of oh, six or so. I invariably made the mince pies at Christmas; it was my special job. And I always helped her in the kitchen. I'd always wanted to eventually be a chef. I couldn't imagine doing anything else. I did do a stint in a solicitor's office, typing legal documents, but I hated it. Then I worked in a restaurant for a while.'

'You've done well. I would imagine your services are in great demand.'

She inclined her head in agreement; she couldn't bring herself to actually utter the lie.

'What does your other half think about all your evening work?'

'Other half?' She frowned. He couldn't mean Max, surely? She doubted he even knew he existed.

'You were with him last evening. The date you mentioned, presumably?'

'Oh, you mean Ben. He's not my other half. We just see each other now and then.'

His other eyebrow went up this time. 'Really? You looked pretty involved when I saw you.'

'When you saw me? You mean in the pub?'

'No, not in the pub. Later, on your way home, I presume. Yours or his?'

She stared at him, puzzled.

'I saw him kissing you, pretty passionately for a man who isn't your other half.'

'He isn't my other half — and for your information, he left me at my door.' She felt a stirring of irritation. Had he been spying on her?

'I drove past you on my way home. You didn't notice me; you were . . . fully occupied.'

'Oh.' She didn't know what to say to that.

'Tell me, do you always do your lovemaking at the side of the road?'

'I wasn't making love.'

'What would you call it, then?'

Kat felt her temper rising, intensifying her already deep irritation. 'If you don't mind me saying so, I can't see what business it is of yours what I do and with whom.'

'I don't mind at all. And you're absolutely right, it's none of my business. So, with that cleared up, can I get you another drink?'

'I don't think so. If we're finished

here, I have to go.'

'Oh? Other clients to see?' And that infernal eyebrow went up again. Who on earth did he think he was, Roger Moore? She glared at it — at him, and declined to answer. 'Or is it — what was his name, Ben? Is he waiting for you?'

'No, he's not, but my mother is.' She clenched her jaw. So much for appearing the professional woman. She'd made it sound as if she were dominated by her mother. How stupid was that? Anger, wholly with herself, made her blurt, 'She's been having more trouble in the shop. Horse manure was pushed through her letterbox last night, so understandably she's nervous.' She got to her feet, snatched up her notepad and catalogue, her pens and her phone, and thrust them all into her bag. She couldn't go on sitting across the table from him a second longer.

He frowned, and his expression was all of a sudden every bit as grim as hers must be. His tone was a harsh one as he said, 'I do hope you're not implying it had anything to do with me. In fact, in your place, I would be very careful indeed about what I said next.'

'Oh, believe me, I am being — will be,' she amended. 'Now, if you still want me to cater your dinner party — ?' Belatedly, she realised she could have fatally jeopardised her chances as far as that was concerned. For sure, he'd now tell her to forget it.

But instead, he said, 'Of course I want you to do it. Why wouldn't I?' A hint of surprise tinged his tone.

She shrugged. 'Well . . . '

'You haven't actually accused me. Of course, if you had,' he smoothly went on, 'that would be an entirely different matter.'

Kat didn't respond. That had sounded like a threat, smoothly voiced or not. A feeling of sick dread quivered through her. If he should hear the rumour about his possible role in the damage done to Petals, he'd surely lay the blame squarely at her feet. And then what would he do?

As if to emphasise his politeness in the face of her insinuation, he asked, 'Do you have your own transport, or can I offer you a lift back? That bag must be heavy, seeing as it contains everything but the kitchen sink.' His voice quivered slightly on the last few words. Amusement, she again wondered, or sarcasm? Probably both, she decided. Well, she wasn't going to rise to either of them.

Managing to maintain a composure she was miles from feeling, she said, 'I walked here so I'm sure I'll be able to walk back.'

'Don't be silly, Kat. It's quite a distance from your mother's shop. You'll dislocate a shoulder or something.'

He was right, of course. Damn him. She had regretted not driving halfway through the journey here. 'Okay,' she grudgingly agreed, 'thank you.'

'Right, come along then.'

She felt like a small girl being chivvied along by an impatient adult.

She scowled as she hefted her bag onto her shoulder.

He grinned and said, 'As I recall, you were pretty stubborn as a girl.'

How the hell did he know that? She'd had no contact with him in those days, apart from overhearing his scornful remark to his friend. She was tempted then to demand whether he also recalled implying she wasn't glamorous enough to merit his admiration. However, she thought better of it. If she pushed him too far, he might just be driven to cancel the dinner party, or at least cancel her part in it. And she needed the money it would earn for her.

They drove the short distance in silence, but just as Kat was climbing from the front passenger seat, Sylvester unexpectedly asked, 'So if this Ben's not your other half, who is?'

'Nobody,' she sharply replied. If it was question time, maybe she should ask about the woman *he'd* been with. 'I don't have the time for any sort of relationship. I'm far too busy working.'

He cocked his head to one side and narrowed his gaze at her. 'There's a vacancy, then?' This was said so casually, so smoothly, the actual words didn't initially register with her.

When they did, she blinked and said, 'Vacancy? For what?' What on earth was he talking about? Vacancy? For the position of what, exactly?

'Boyfriend, lover, other half — whatever you want to call it.'

'F-for me, do you mean?'

'Yes.' Quivers of what looked maddeningly like amusement again tugged at his mouth.

Was he laughing at her? Yet again amusing himself by toying with her, trying to get some sort of reaction from her? She decided to let him have it. 'Why? Are you applying?' she snapped, her expression daring him to say yes.

'Could be,' he drawled, his voice deepening as he held her gaze with his.

'Hah! Don't bother. I haven't got the

time, as I've just said, and . . . and . . . '
She didn't know what else to say to
him. His response had been the very
last thing she'd expected.

'And, and, what?'

Not content with amusing himself at
her expense, he was now provocatively
mimicking her. Well, she'd show him.
Kat Lucas was not someone to be
messed with. 'I'm not interested; not in
you, not in any man.'

'Why? You're not gay, are you?'

She was almost too furious now to
respond — almost. 'No,' she managed
to grind out. 'Why would you think that
just because I'm not interested in you,
I'd be interested in women?'

He shrugged, a strange expression
now lighting his eyes. If she hadn't
known better, she'd have said it was
hurt. 'I don't usually get turned down,'
he quietly said.

She took a deep breath and muttered, 'No, I'm sure you don't, but I'm
not like other women.'

He gave a shout of laughter and she

ruefully conceded that she'd played right into his hands. She'd more or less admitted to being unlike other women because she was gay. Which, of course, she wasn't.

'Calm down,' he said. 'I'm teasing you.' But then the laughter faded as swiftly as it had arisen. 'After all, I witnessed that kiss last night. You clearly like men, just not me.' Again, he cocked his head and regarded her. 'Which is a great pity. I think we'd be good together.'

She was aghast and didn't bother to hide it. 'We'd be good together?' She snorted a laugh. 'No, we wouldn't. I'd never get together with a wrecker like you.'

'A wrecker? Me?' He looked genuinely astonished.

'That's what you're planning to do, isn't it? To wreck people's lives. My mother's life, for one, and Charlie Turnbull's next door. This shop,' she said, pointing backwards to Petals, 'is Mum's life. She bought it after my father's death, and she's worked tirelessly and single-handedly to build her customer base. And you — you come along and just want to pull it all down; destroy all her efforts. You're even prepared to — ' She stopped just in time. His features had darkened ominously, his mouth compressed into a straight line. His eyes were almost black; a menacing black.

'Well, don't stop there. Prepared to what, exactly?' His expression once more threatened her, warning her to be very, very careful.

'I have to go. Perhaps you'd confirm the matters we discussed? That's if you still want me.'

'Oh, I still want you,' he murmured throatily. 'Even more now. I do like a woman with spirit. Goodnight, Kat. I'll be in touch.'

He grinned at her as he toed the ignition. The engine roared. Kat hastily slammed the door shut and stood staring after him as he sped down the road.

What the hell had he meant — he still wanted her, even more now? Had he meant as a caterer, or something much more intimate? And where did that leave his companion of the evening before?

5

That night someone pushed a lit firework through the shop letterbox. Fortunately Kat was still in the kitchen, which was next door to Ruth's bedroom and immediately above the shop, which was why she heard the snap of the letterbox and then the initial bangs of the firework. She ran to the window and was just in time to see a figure disappearing into the darkness.

She quickly opened the window and leaned out, but the person had vanished. She had managed to catch a glimpse, however, of a long, dark coat and wide-brimmed hat, just as Ruth had described. She ran from the kitchen shouting, 'Mum, Mum, someone has pushed something through the letterbox again,' before heading for the stairs.

The acrid smell of something burning was the first thing to reach her; then she was racing into the shop. She spotted the firework immediately, snapping and smoking just inside the door. Fortunately it wasn't close enough to anything to start a fire. She ran across to it and stamped it out before going into the storeroom, to the sink, and filling a bucket with water. She ran back and doused the firework.

By that time, Ruth had arrived. 'Kat, oh God, what's burning?'

'A firework. I've doused it with water, so it's safe.'

'Thank goodness you were here. I was asleep and didn't hear a thing. The whole place could have burned down with me in it.' She gave a little sob.

'I know,' Kat grimly said.

'I'll ring the police.' Ruth went to the phone. 'They'll have to do something now.'

★   ★   ★

Again, it was Paul who turned up. Kat described what had happened. 'I'm sorry; I know it's not much help. Whoever it was had gone almost at once. He didn't look very tall, though. I did manage to see that. Five foot eight or nine, maybe. It's just a guess.'

'Could it have been Brett Sinclair?' Ruth put in.

'No, he's taller than five eight,' Kat said.

Ruth regarded her quizzically. 'You've seen him?'

'Yes, the other night in the pub.'

'Did you speak to him?'

'I was with Daisy.' Her response was an evasive one, but Ruth didn't seem to notice. Or did she?

'How did you know it was him?' Ruth's tone was one of almost accusation.

'He was with Sylvester Jordan.' Kat shrugged, not quite able to meet her mother's eyes. 'So it seemed a natural assumption to make.' She dared not tell her mother that it had been Sylvester himself who'd introduced them. Now wasn't the time. Mind you, she didn't know when would be. She chewed at her lower lip. Ruth was still staring at her, her gaze now a deeply suspicious one. However, she said no more.

'Who's Brett Sinclair?' Paul asked.

'He works with Sylvester Jordan. In what capacity exactly, I'm not sure.'

'Are you saying you think the incidents are down to Jordan?'

'We have no evidence of that,' Kat guardedly said, 'but it does seem reasonable to suspect that he could be the one behind it all. It didn't look like either him or Brett Sinclair, though. Whoever it was wasn't big enough.' Again, she was aware of her mother's stare. Something occurred to her then. Something that would hopefully distract Ruth and prevent her from putting two and two together and coming up with the correct answer — that Kat had indeed been speaking to Sylvester. Had, in fact, agreed to cater for him. 'I wonder if Charlie's been attacked too?

We ought to make sure he's okay.'

'I'll go,' Paul said. 'Has he had the same thing happening? He hasn't reported anything.'

'As far as we know, he hasn't,' Kat said slowly, frowning as she did so. Why hadn't his shop been targeted too? It wasn't just Ruth that Jordan Enterprises wanted out. 'Maybe something frightens whoever it is away before they get to Charlie.'

Paul was quickly back. 'The shop's in darkness and I can't see any damage. I'll call back in the morning and have a word with him.'

'It's beginning to look as if it's just my mother who's being targeted,' Kat said.

'Yes, it does,' Paul answered. 'Perhaps whoever's doing this thinks because she's a woman on her own, she'll be more easily intimidated than a man would be. And if she gives up the fight, then the likelihood is so will Charlie. He won't want to be the only one left.'

Once Paul had gone, promising to

get a police vehicle to drive past both shops on a nightly basis — which partially satisfied Ruth, for the moment at any rate — Kat and her mother sat together in the kitchen, drinking hot chocolate and talking about what was happening. To Kat's relief, Ruth didn't pursue her line of questioning about whether Kat had spoken to Sylvester and Brett Sinclair, though she suspected that Ruth had begun to guess there was more to her daughter's sighting of the two men in the pub than she was letting on.

'Do you think Paul's right, and I'm being specifically targeted because I'm a woman on my own?' Ruth asked.

'It sounds a reasonable supposition. What does Charlie say about what's happening?'

The phone rang, interrupting their conversation. 'Who can that be at this time of night?' Ruth muttered, getting up to answer it. 'Hello? Ruth Lucas speaking.' As she listened to whoever it was at the other end, her face paled alarmingly and she cried, 'Who is this? Who? Leave me alone, do you hear?'

Kat, troubled by the look on her mother's face, also got to her feet. She grabbed the phone. 'Who is this? Hello? Hello?' But there was only silence. The caller had rung off. She immediately dialled 1471, only to be told that the caller's number had been withheld.

She replaced the receiver and looked at Ruth. 'What did he say?'

'That I've been warned, and now it's time to go before something more serious happens. Oh Kat, I'm scared, really scared.'

'It was definitely a man?' Of course it was a man. No woman would do something like this.

'I-I think so. I don't know. The voice was strange, muffled, as if the person was holding something over their mouth. But no, I'm sure it was a man. It has to be Sylvester Jordan behind it. Who else would have any reason to do this? And why just pick on me?'

Next morning, Kat could see how exhausted her mother was. She obviously hadn't slept at all. They'd decided after a great deal of discussion the evening before not to ring the police again. 'After all,' Kat had argued, 'what can they do? They're not going to use up precious resources trying to identify the caller. Have a day off, Mum. Try and forget it all.'

Ruth snorted. 'Forget it all? Fat chance.'

Undaunted, Kat went on, 'I know it'll be difficult. But go and do some shopping. Treat yourself. I'll look after the shop.'

'No, I can't.'

'Yes you can, and it'll make a change for me. Take my mind off my problems too, and I've got nothing better to do. Go on, dress up and go spend some money. A bit of retail therapy will be just the thing.'

Eventually, and with a great deal of

reluctance, Ruth agreed, and Kat was left alone. She was halfway through the morning newspaper when a woman walked in — a slim, very attractive and well-dressed woman. Her cream linen dress and jacket screamed designer-made, as did her coffee-coloured shoes and handbag. Her skilfully made-up face was exquisite, and her hair was professionally styled. All in all, she could easily have graced the silver screen or even the catwalk.

'Oh,' she exclaimed, 'I was expecting to see Mrs Lucas. You obviously aren't her. Too young.'

'I'm her daughter, Kat. She's gone out for a while. I'm standing in for her, so how can I help you?'

'Well, I was hoping for a confidential word with her, but maybe it's better if I talk to you. You could perhaps exert some influence upon her.'

Kat almost laughed out loud at that. Exert influence on her mother? That would be the day. Her mother very much went her own way, and anyone who tried to convince her to do otherwise got very short shrift. Look how hard she'd resisted the idea of leaving her shop under Kat's steward-ship to go shopping.

'I'm Maria Jordan, wife of Oscar, mother of Sylvester.' She spoke as if she were making some sort of royal proclamation to her loyal subjects.

Kat fleetingly wondered if she was expected to curtsey. Hastily, she smoth-ered a giggle and instead managed to say, 'I don't really have much influence over my mother. Why do you ask?'

Maria Jordan glanced around the shop, her expression one of superiority. 'I have to say, I can see why these places need to be pulled down and something more sophisticated built in their place. It would be so beneficial to this neighbourhood.' She wrinkled her dainty nose. 'Yet your mother's stub-bornly refusing to move out.'

'Not just my mother,' Kat said. 'Charlie Turnbull's also standing firm. The shop next door,' she said in response to the other woman's quizzical stare.

'Yes, I do know. But really, my dear, wouldn't your mother and — um, Mr Turnbull — be better off in nice new shops? Something more modern, more convenient?' She snorted disparagingly, allowing her glance to roam round again, lingering as it did so on the shelves that were desperately in need of a coat of paint, the worn linoleum floor, the cramped counter, the array of well-used buckets containing ready-wrapped arrangements of flowers. 'This is holding up all of my son's plans.' With a condescending smile, she continued, 'He's getting a little exasperated with it all. But then, I expect you're thinking, what's it to do with me?'

'Precisely.'

She looked taken aback at Kat's peremptory tone. 'I'll wait and have a little chat with your mother. I'm sure she'll see sense.'

'I wouldn't bet on it,' Kat muttered

beneath her breath. 'And there's no point in waiting. She won't be back for hours.'

'Oh.' Her expression conveyed her annoyance at what Kat had told her. She obviously wasn't accustomed to being told she couldn't have exactly what she wanted when she wanted it. Kat could see now where Sylvester got his high-handedness from. 'Well, while I'm here, I'll take some flowers. Something different, not the usual mediocre mixed bunch.' Her tone poured scorn on the flowers that sat all around the shop. 'What can you offer me?'

Kat had to think quickly. She wasn't familiar with all that her mother had in stock. 'We have some late sunflowers.'

'Oh dear me, no. So vulgar, I always think. So brash.'

Kat smothered another giggle. What a dreadful woman. Once more, she decided that it was no wonder Sylvester was like he was. She wondered if his father was the same. 'Um, well, we have lilies, roses of course, and then there's these. I'm not sure what they are.' Mind you, she'd probably consider these vulgar too, with their long stems and large, showy blooms.

'Do you know, I think I'll leave it.' She paused and belatedly gave Kat a long, hard look. 'Are you by any chance the Kat of Katering For U?'

'That's me,' Kat cheerily said.

'You're going to be cooking for my son, aren't you?'

'That's right.'

'He did mention you were the daughter of the woman in the flower shop. I'm surprised he's using you, frankly.'

'Are you?' Kat said.

'Well, yes.' She stopped short of putting it into actual words, but Kat had no trouble guessing what she'd almost said. *Seeing as it's your mother who's giving him so much trouble.* Instead, she went on, 'Are you quite sure you couldn't persuade your mother?'

'Positive. And maybe you should tell whoever's concerned that no amount of intimidation and vandalism is going to convince her to move out.'

The older woman stared back at her. 'I really have no idea what you're talking about.'

'No? Then maybe you should ask — ' She stopped abruptly. It might not be wise to all but accuse her son, especially if she should take it into her head to repeat Kat's words to Sylvester. It could, despite what Sylvester had said, lose her the only job she'd got at the moment, and that was the last thing she needed.

* * *

That evening Sylvester himself rang Kat on her mobile phone, confirming that it would be twelve people for dinner.

'Fine. I can start planning, and order the ingredients. Oh, by the way,' she couldn't resist adding, 'your mother came into Petals today, looking for some flowers.'

'Did she?' He sounded surprised.

'Yes, and then she tried to get me to

persuade my mother to move out.'

'That wasn't at my behest.' He sounded vexed. 'I'll have a word with her.'

'Maybe you could also find out who it was who pushed a lit firework through the shop letterbox last night. They could have burned the place down with my mother and me inside.' Her anger wouldn't be contained any longer, even though she knew was risking the most lucrative job she'd had in a good while.

'What?'

'I'm sure you heard me.'

'Kat, no one that I employ would do such a thing.'

'Are you absolutely sure of that?'

There was a momentary silence, and then he said, 'Has it ever occurred to you that it could all be down to an out-of-control, disaffected youth? There are always incidents like this around at this time of year.'

'I saw the person responsible,' she told him, 'and it didn't look like a youth. No youth that I know of would wear a long overcoat and a wide-brimmed hat. He'd be much more likely to be dressed in a hoodie, with a scarf wrapped round the lower part of his face. No, this is no youth simply out to cause damage to property, anyone's property, just for the hell of it; this is someone deliberately targeting my mother.'

'I assume from the way you've described it that you couldn't see this person's face. In which case, how can you be so sure that it's someone who works for me?'

His tone was such that it left her in no doubt of what the consequences would be if she actually accused him of being the one behind these offences, which she wasn't about to do. She'd seen for herself that it wasn't him. The perpetrator hadn't been tall enough. But she couldn't rid herself of the idea that he could have been the one to instigate it.

'All I know is that it's someone out to

intimidate and terrify her into leaving. Oh yes, and she also had an anonymous late-night phone call telling her she'd had her warning, and now it was time to leave.' And that, she decided, could well have been Sylvester.

He was beginning to sound exasperated, rather than angry as she'd expected. 'Kat, it wasn't anything to do with me. You have my word.'

'Your word. Right.' She knew she sounded scathing about his insistence that he wasn't the person responsible for everything, but she simply couldn't help herself.

But he must have decided to ignore that, because he went on to ask, for all the world as if the heated exchange had never taken place, 'So back to business — what time should I expect you for the dinner party preparations?'

⋆ ⋆ ⋆

After that, the day of the dinner party came round all too quickly for Kat.

Sylvester was the last person she would have chosen to cater for, especially as Daisy wasn't free to assist her. She was going to have to manage alone, and as fate would have it, it had to be her most complicated menu.

She'd considered asking her mother for help, at least for the evening, but Ruth still didn't know who she was about to cook for and Kat hadn't been able to face the row that would inevitably erupt once she did know. And even if she agreed to help, Kat couldn't be sure that she wouldn't blurt out her accusations about Sylvester in front of his guests. Maybe Sylvester's housekeeper would help out — for a fee, of course.

All of which made her set out for Linford Manor earlier than she normally would have, in the hope that the extra time would allow her to make up for the lack of any help.

The manor house was situated a couple of miles out of the town, so it didn't take Kat long to get there.

Although she knew where it was, she'd never before ventured beyond the imposing eight-foot-high wrought-iron gates. These were flanked by an equally high, densely planted hawthorn and holly hedgerow that ran as far as the eye could see in each direction and presumably marked out the perimeter of the grounds. As a consequence, she couldn't see the actual building.

She drove slowly and slightly nervously along a driveway that was lengthy, and meandered between a border of trees and thick shrubs to be finally confronted by the sight of the house itself. Her mouth dropped open as she crunched to a halt on the deeply gravelled circular forecourt. It had to be the most elegant building she'd ever seen. In fact, it could realistically have come straight out of the pages of one of her favourite Jane Austen novels, *Pride and Prejudice*. Constructed in rose-coloured brick, it was three storeys high with a steeply sloping grey slate roof and a battalion of ornamental chimneys. Rows of mullioned windows lay beneath all of this, the glass panes gleaming as they reflected the morning sunlight. A short flight of shallow stone steps led up to a magnificent oak door.

A middle-aged woman opened it in response to Kat's rather tentative ringing of the bell. 'Yes?' Her tone could in no way be described as a welcoming one. In fact, frigid would have been the most apt adjective.

'Katering For U.' Kat smiled at her, hoping to warm things up a little. The tactic failed miserably.

The woman merely sniffed and looked Kat up and down as if she were something the dog was about to drag in on its paw. 'Would you go round the back? You can unload your things straight into the kitchen. I don't want it all carted through my clean hallway.'

'Oh right, yes. That's good, easier for me.'

But the door had already been closed on her.

'Okaaay, so that's how things are going to be,' she muttered. 'No help forthcoming there, then.'

Half an hour later, she was installed in one of the largest and most comprehensively fitted kitchens she'd ever seen; her own pots and pans were spread out along just one of the worktops. She usually brought a few of her most used and favourite pieces of equipment with her, just in case. Another of the remaining three surfaces was covered with the ingredients she'd need for the meal. And still there was heaps of space. The housekeeper had watched her closely throughout, but she hadn't offered to help.

Kat finally turned to her and with outstretched hand said, 'I'm Kat.'

'I pretty much guessed that.' The woman's expression was one of hostility; her stance was stiffly erect, her arms crossed over her chest.

'And you are?'

'Joan, Joan White.' Her tone was every bit as stiff as her bearing.

'Housekeeper to Mr Sylvester.'

Kat felt her spirits nosedive. Oh God, this was going to be sheer hell, she just knew it. 'Nice to meet you, Joan. I'll try not to get in your way.'

'You're already in my way. I need to begin preparing lunch for the family.'

From then on, it all rapidly went downhill. For, large kitchen or not, and deliberately or not, the housekeeper ensured she was standing in the way wherever Kat turned.

In the end Kat was compelled to say quite forcibly, 'Look, Mr Jordan is paying me to prepare a meal for twelve this evening. If you have a problem with that, please take it up with him. But I really do need some space, otherwise I'm not going to have it ready by eight o'clock.'

'Everything okay in here?'

It was Sylvester. Kat found herself breathing a sigh of heartfelt relief, and she'd never expected to ever feel that as far as he was concerned. She wondered — no, hoped — he'd overheard her words of complaint. She suspected he had, because he took immediate charge of the appreciably tense situation.

'Joan, I wonder if you'd go and lay the table for me. You're so good at that. We're going to be using the large dining room. The flowers for the centrepiece have just been delivered; they're in the pantry.' He smiled at the housekeeper, and her previously stiff demeanour vanished as if someone had waved a magic wand.

'Of course, Mr Sylvester. I'd be pleased to.'

'And then take the rest of the afternoon off. I'm sure Ms Lucas can manage.'

'Right you are. I'll be off, then. Table first, then the flowers.'

Kat watched her leave, unable to conceal her gratitude.

'She's good at heart,' Sylvester said. 'She simply hates feeling she's not up to certain tasks. But a meal for twelve would have been stretching her capabilities a bit too far.' He smiled warmly.

Clearly their row over the various incidents in her mother's shop had been put to one side, if not forgotten — at least for today. 'How are you coping? No help today? I thought you had an assistant.'

'I do, but she had something else on. So it's just me, I'm afraid.'

'Oh please, don't be afraid. I'm sure you'll cope admirably. Now, I've put your costume in one of the bedrooms.'

She stared at him, quite unable to hide her horror.

His silver-grey eyes twinkled. 'I'm kidding. I'm sure you'll be appropriately attired. But I don't want you to serve at table. In fact, I'd like you to join us to eat, if that could be arranged.'

Kat once again stared at him. 'Oh no, really, I couldn't. I like to serve the food, clear up and go. And without Daisy . . . ' She shrugged.

'I'm sure we can manage without Daisy. The guests won't mind helping themselves. I'd really appreciate you joining us. It would make up the numbers at the table. One of the guests has had to cancel — Esther. You probably saw her with me the other evening at the Latimers' and then in the Green Frog.'

He must mean his glamorous companion; the one who'd assumed ownership over him — or so it had appeared to Kat. Desperate to come up with an acceptable excuse not to have to do as he asked, she blurted the only reason she could think of. 'I don't have anything suitable to wear.' She indicated her working attire of jeans and shirt. She'd left a smarter outfit in the van, which she'd planned to put on for the serving of the guests: a navy-blue pencil skirt and pristine white blouse. Her choice had been made in a deliberate attempt to emphasise the contrast to the French maid's outfit at the Latimers' dinner.

'Oh, I see.' He eyed her. 'Is that the only reason you won't join us?'

She was tempted to say, 'No. The truth is I don't fancy sitting down with any guests of yours. They're bound to be as arrogant and self-satisfied as you are.' However, she made do with a rather feeble, 'Well . . . '

'You could pop home, couldn't you?' He raised an eyebrow at her. It seemed a favourite trick of his, brought into play for all sorts of reasons; sometimes to put the pressure on, while at other times simply to charm. This time it was to charm and thus get his own way. 'I could keep an eye on things here for you.'

'You?' She couldn't disguise her surprise.

'Oh yes,' he airily said. 'I have been known to cook a meal for friends. I'm not completely useless in the kitchen. Please.' He gazed at her almost beseechingly. 'You'd really be doing me a gigantic favour.'

6

She didn't really know how, but Kat found herself returning to her flat once the meal was more or less ready, apart from a few last-minute tasks, and hurriedly shampooed her hair before changing into one of only two dresses she owned that were in any way suitable for formal dining. She was much more into smart casual wear.

The dress, however, was Kat's favourite; the colour of caramel toffee to bring out the hazel of her eyes, it had a low, rounded neckline, a fitted bodice, and a gently flared skirt that reached to just above her knees. Cream-coloured high-heeled shoes and a matching clutch bag completed the outfit. She eyed herself in the mirror. Was it dressy enough, or would the black one be better? It certainly had a higher neckline. This one exposed the tops of her breasts, but in no way could it be compared to the maid's costume she'd worn at the Latimers'.

It would have to do, she decided; she didn't have enough time to change again. She set about arranging her hair, deftly piling it up onto the top of her head in a spiky arrangement, and leaving just a few strands free to curl around and frame her face.

Eventually, satisfied that she'd done the best she could in the time that she had, she returned to Linford Manor to discover Sylvester in the kitchen, conscientiously monitoring the progress of everything just as he'd promised. Fortunately, the kitchen possessed a bank of ovens, one of which was for warming. She'd already cooked a lot of the dishes and placed them inside. There they would remain until they were needed.

Sylvester turned and looked at her as she entered the room. His gaze, as it had a disconcerting habit of doing, raked her from head to foot — and wouldn't you know it, an unwanted strand of hair chose that particular moment to work itself free and drop down over her eyes. She silently swore and fixed it back up. Almost at once it dropped again.

Sylvester grinned. 'Leave it,' he said. 'It looks great. Positively seductive, in fact.' He grinned, this time even more broadly.

Kat frowned at him. Seductive was the very last effect she'd wanted; it made her even more wary about joining the guests at the table. The women were sure to be the glossy, sophisticated types that she invariably felt uncomfortable with. They'd be dressed to the nines in designer outfits, making her efforts seem totally inadequate. Making *her* seem inadequate.

'You look . . . ' His eyes roamed over her a second time in a deliberate and provocative leisurely fashion, the warmth in them intensifying as they went. ' . . . lovely.'

Kat felt her cheeks reddening. Had

her neckline slipped? She glanced down. No, it was precisely where she'd left it.

'Nothing's moved or slipped,' he said teasingly. 'It's all just perfect. You'll put the other women to shame, I'm sure.'

Huh! She wished. She had a feeling that she'd appear sadly underdressed in what would, as she'd already decided, be much more glamorous company.

'Well th-thank you,' she haltingly said. 'I'll just finish off in here.'

He checked the clock on the wall. 'Right, I'm off to change. I've invited everyone for seven thirty. Could you join us then?'

'I doubt it. There's several last-minutes things I need to do.'

'Okay. Well, if you could make it as soon as possible. Joan has agreed to bring the food in for us between courses.'

Kat couldn't hide her astonishment.

'I've had a word with her. She returned while you were at home changing. She'll clear up too, so you can relax and enjoy yourself.'

'Relax? Enjoy myself?' she echoed. 'You're not paying me to relax and enjoy myself. You're paying me a not inconsiderable amount of money to prepare a meal and serve it.'

He shrugged as if that were inconsequential. Maybe it was, to someone as wealthy as he was. 'Yes, and you will have more than earned it. The food is looking fabulous.' He indicated the array of dishes that were spread out ready to serve. 'Joan doesn't mind. She likes to be involved.'

Kat doubted that, if it meant being involved with her. She narrowed her eyes and asked, 'She doesn't mind? Are you sure of that?'

'Kat, it's what I pay her for.' And he shrugged again. 'By the way, the guest bedrooms are always kept prepared, so if you want to, you can stay the night.'

'Oh no,' she instantly said. 'My mother's expecting me back.'

A quizzical eyebrow lifted at her.

'She's grown increasingly nervous

after the recent attacks on the shop.' Her attempt to justify her previous remark fell onto stony ground. For Sylvester's good-looking features had darkened and hardened.

'Whatever's happened,' he rasped, 'I promise you, it is not down to me. Please believe that.'

And, against all the odds, Kat belatedly found that she did.

By the time Joan returned to the kitchen, her expression considerably less hostile, Kat had done everything that could be in done in advance.

'Okay, I'll join Sylvester and his guests for a little while, then I'll come back and warm the quiches.'

'Um, if you tell me what to do, I could see to that and then bring them all into the dining room for you,' Joan unexpectedly offered.

Kat eyed her uncertainly.

'You needn't worry, Ms Lucas. I'll do exactly as you say.'

'Please, call me Kat.'

'And I'm Joan.' The housekeeper

held out a hand. 'I'm sorry I was less than welcoming this morning.'

'Oh, please, it's forgotten.' Again, she looked at the housekeeper. 'Well, if you're sure — '

'I am. You tell me how you want things and I'll do all that's necessary in here. You can join the party. I know that's what Mr Sylvester wants.'

Kat wondered what 'Mr Sylvester' had said to her to make her so amenable. Whatever it was, it had worked. She carefully explained to Joan what had to be done with the first two courses. 'I'll pop out though, if that's okay, to finish off the steaks. I don't wish to impose on you.'

'You won't. I'd like to help. I might even pick up a few tips; you never know.' She smiled warmly.

Kat returned the smile. 'I'll also do the crêpes Suzette.'

Relief brightened Joan's eyes. 'That's the one thing I was really worried about.'

'Okay, that's sorted then.' She removed

the apron she'd put on to protect her dress. 'If there's any sort of problem, come and get me — please.'

'I will, don't you worry about that. Now, off you go and enjoy yourself.'

'Um — where will they all be?' She realised she had no idea of the layout of the rest of the house.

Joan beamed and proceeded to issue some very detailed instructions.

Kat walked nervously into the large, almost baronial hallway — it even contained a minstrel's gallery, she saw — and counted the doors leading off. Joan had said the sitting room, where everyone would be having pre-dinner drinks, was the third door on the left.

As Kat neared it, the sounds of several voices and much laughter reached her. Her already jangling nerves intensified their dance. In a bid to calm them, she smoothed the skirt of her dress down over her rounded hips, and then put up a hand to check her hair was still tidy. Joan had told her that there was a cloakroom to the left of the front door. Maybe she should just pop in and make sure she was presentable.

Before she could do so, however, the door to the sitting room opened and Sylvester strode out. 'Ah, I was just coming to fetch you.' As it invariably did, his glance slid over her, making her fingers itch to check out her unruly hair. 'Come along,' he said, holding out a hand to her. 'I'll introduce you to everyone.'

She was growing more apprehensive by the second; so much so, she was sure she could feel herself actually trembling. She took his hand, praying he wouldn't detect her misgivings.

'No need to look so nervous,' he murmured. 'I promise I won't eat you.'

Kat stared up at him. His gleaming eyes snagged hers. He wouldn't eat her? All of a sudden, she wasn't sure about that. There was a particularly hungry look to him.

He drew her into an impressively large sitting room. It was decorated in shades of ivory, lemon and duck-egg blue. Huge cream settees and chairs, all deeply cushioned, sat around, interspersed with low tables. What looked like a genuine Adam fireplace sat against one wall, a fire burning in it, while watercolour and oil paintings punctuated the remaining walls. Ornate gilt-legged side tables held valuable-looking ornaments. In fact, the whole room screamed immense wealth.

'Now, everyone, let me introduce the star of the evening.'

Kat looked at Sylvester in horror. The star of the evening? Hardly. She was simply the cook.

'This is Kat, who's entirely responsible for the gorgeous feast you're about to eat.' He swivelled his head to look at her, his gaze an extraordinarily warm one. 'Kat, I'd like you to meet — ' And he reeled off a list of names which vanished from her head the second he'd uttered them. She'd never been good at names. Faces, yes; but names — forget them. Which, sadly, she did on a regular basis.

'And finally, my oldest friend, Dan Woodward, with his wife, Elaine. You might remember Dan from school.'

Kat did remember him. He'd been the most terrible flirt; no girl had been safe within six inches of him. He'd even tried it on in a half-hearted sort of way with Kat once, as she recalled. She doubted he'd remember, though. She hoped he'd changed, otherwise she pitied his wife.

She smiled now and said, 'I think I do remember you.' She then turned to his wife and asked, 'Were you at the same school?'

Elaine pointedly raised her perfectly plucked eyebrows and said, 'Good gracious, no. I went to school in Cheltenham. I lived there then, and my parents still do.'

Kat belatedly became aware of Dan's intent stare. 'I think I remember you,' he went on to say. 'You looked a bit different in those days.' It was more than evident that he approved of the change. She saw his wife glance sharply at him. 'You were a shy little thing, as I recall.'

So he did remember her. 'Well, I've grown up since then,' Kat said.

'Yes, I can see that,' he said, again admiringly. 'You obviously remember her too, Vester?'

'Oh yes,' Sylvester drawled. 'I remember her, very well as a matter of fact. As I recall, she batted you away very efficiently.' He smiled grimly at his friend.

Kat looked at him, wondering if that was all he remembered, or if he also remembered how scornfully he himself had dismissed her. If not, maybe she should remind him.

But the moment passed, and he was asking her what she wanted to drink. 'We're all on champagne.'

'That would be perfect,' she replied. 'What are you celebrating?'

Elaine Woodward gave a tinkle of a laugh. 'Oh dear me, where have you been, my dear? These days we don't need to be celebrating to drink champagne. Why, I have a glass most days. It bucks me up no end.'

If all of that was said to put Kat firmly in her place — and she rather thought that after her husband's reaction to Kat, it had been — it worked. She instantly felt gauche and unworldly. This was exactly why she preferred to be in the kitchen. She hated pretension and snobbery. *We're all the same under our exteriors*, she reassured herself, though clearly Elaine considered herself way too superior to be mixing with the lowly kitchen staff. *Maybe I ought to act the part and assume a yokel accent*, Kat thought scathingly.

Before she could give in to temptation, however, Sylvester was holding out a flute of what tasted like very expensive champagne. He smiled almost tenderly at her; he'd obviously heard what Elaine had said. One of the other women must have felt the same way, because she came to speak to Kat. She was considerably older, which perhaps was why she was being so kind.

'So tell me, Kat, do you do this on a regular basis?'

'Oh, yes. I've got my own catering business.'

'Have you? I'm full of admiration. I've never been very good at any sort of business. Do you always cater for private dinner parties?'

Kat nodded. 'Mostly. Though I'm thinking of trying to move into the corporate side of catering. You know — cater for business functions, doing things on a larger and more commercial scale.' It sounded grand and maybe a tad pretentious, but it was an aspect of what she did that she'd only recently begun to consider. Somehow she had to drum up more work, or go under.

'How fantastic, and so enterprising of you. If you've got a card, I'd like one. I do envy anyone who can cook well. I'm useless.'

The man who was her husband laughed fondly and said, 'I can testify to that, but I love her anyway.' And it was clear he did, if the way he looked at her was anything to judge by.

Once the woman returned to her husband, Kat said to Sylvester, 'Dan called you Vester.'

'Yes, it's what all my friends call me. Only my family, my mother in particular, insist on addressing me by my full name. Oh, and my older sister, Alexis.'

'I'd forgotten you had a sister. Where is she now?'

'In the States. She married an American and now has two children, a boy and a girl. She and my mother both refuse to use the shortened version of my name. My mother says it sounds like some sort of undergarment.' He smiled wryly.

Kat laughed. 'Well, I suppose she could be right. It does rather.'

'That's the first time I've heard you laugh, really laugh. You should do it more often.' His gaze lingered on her mouth. It was as if he were touching her; caressing her. 'And please,' he softly went on, 'call me Vester too. I do actually prefer it.'

Thoroughly unnerved by this display of intimacy and admiration, Kat took a large mouthful of her champagne, only to instantly splutter on the sheer quantity of bubbles that sprang into the back of her throat.

'Steady now,' Sylvester cautioned. 'Are you all right?'

Her eyes were watering and everyone was staring at her. Once again, she felt unsophisticated and gauche. It must be evident to them all that she wasn't accustomed to drinking champagne.

'What on earth did you say to her, Vester?' the man who'd been introduced as another old friend of Sylvester's, John somebody-or-other, said. 'You want to watch him, Kat. He fancies himself as a real ladies' man.'

'John,' the woman at his side admonished him. 'Ignore him, Kat. Vester is always a perfect gentleman.'

At which point, and to Kat's huge relief, Joan walked into the room and announced, 'Mr Sylvester, dinner is served.'

7

Sylvester himself escorted Kat into the dining room and led her to a seat at the table. The mini-quiches were already at each place setting, perfectly arranged upon their beds of dressed rocket and watercress leaves. Sylvester sat at the head of the table, to the right of her. The remaining ten people seated themselves wherever they wanted. Kat was mildly surprised at this, expecting someone like Sylvester to have arranged a more formal seating plan.

Everyone immediately began eating, so it was a few moments before Elaine leaned over the table and said to Kat, 'I could never be a cook, especially for someone else. Goodness,' she remarked, 'I don't even cook for myself and Dan.'

'Really?' one of the other women cut in. 'Who does the cooking for you?'

'Oh, Stella.' Elaine gave a tinkle of a laugh. 'We eat out, of course. Either that, or it's a takeaway — isn't it, darling?' She glanced across at Dan, who was beginning to look resigned and almost weary.

'Yes, dear,' was all he said.

Elaine swept her glance back to Kat. 'What inspired you to take up a career in cooking?' Her nose didn't quite turn up, but it looked for all the world as if she'd had a particularly unpleasant smell waved beneath it. 'Surely you could have found something a little more *interesting*, or ambitious, to do with yourself?'

'It is interesting — to me. And my ambition always was to get into the catering business. It's all I've ever wanted to do.'

'How very quaint. How did you find Kat again, Vester?' she asked. 'Or have you kept in touch since your school-days?'

'No, we haven't, sad to say. She was catering for a dinner party I was invited to and I was so impressed with the food, I asked her to do the same for me. She hasn't disappointed.' He slanted a smile at Kat, as if trying to shield her from Elaine's caustic remarks.

'I'll say she hasn't,' one of the male guests called from the end of the table. 'That was marvellous.' He placed his cutlery neatly on his empty plate.

Elaine, however, wasn't to be side-tracked. She was determined to have her say, that was more than evident. 'But is it usual for the caterer to be invited to sit down at the table and eat with the rest of the guests?' She snorted with what sounded like contemptuous amusement.

Kat, by now, bristling with indignation, couldn't stop herself from saying, 'No, you're right, it's not usual. But Sylvester — Vester — insisted.'

Elaine promptly turned her attention to Sylvester. 'Really? Insisted? How very strange. Is that what people do nowadays — invite the help to join them?' She gave another tinkly laugh.

However, Sylvester didn't appear to be listening. He was talking to the woman on his other side, the older woman who'd kindly come to Kat's aid earlier. But then he unexpectedly swivelled his head and remarked, 'Not that strange, Elaine. As you all know, I employ a housekeeper, Joan; and as she agreed to help out with the serving, I asked Kat to join us all. After working so hard all day, I thought it was the least I could do.' He paused meaningfully. 'And I didn't really think anyone would object.' He left the words *apart from you, Elaine* unsaid, which left no one in any doubt that he'd heard Elaine's every spiteful word.

Elaine's eyes glittered with exasperation at this, but it didn't stop her from retorting somewhat bitterly, 'Well, I suppose as you ended up a guest short, it has served a useful purpose.' However, Sylvester's implied rebuke did have the desired effect, and she finally fell silent. Dan, on the other hand, was looking extremely embarrassed. As for Kat, she was immensely relieved, because she knew she would have replied in kind sooner or later. She only took so much rudeness from anyone.

The rest of the evening passed without further acrimony, the other guests proving pleasantly agreeable. No one made any comment on Kat's disappearance every now and then as she went into the kitchen to assist Joan, and the compliments she received at the end of the evening meant she managed to hand out several of her cards, a couple to men who ran their own businesses and seemed keen to hire her for the corporate catering she'd mentioned. All in all it was a very worthwhile evening, and she hoped it would bring her some much-needed work. And, judging by Sylvester's expression as everyone left, it was exactly what he'd had in mind too. Could he have guessed how little work she had for the foreseeable future? She rather thought he had — and strangely, she didn't mind.

With everyone gone, Kat made a point of thanking Joan for her magnificent efforts before she retired for the night. The housekeeper's chest had swelled with pride and she'd said, 'I thoroughly enjoyed it. It's been a whole new experience for me. If you're ever here again, I'll do the same. You just ask — don't be afraid.'

Then Kat went into the hall to retrieve her coat from the cloakroom. Her boxes of cooking paraphernalia were already stowed away in her van — something else Joan had done for her. Never had first impressions been more wrong, she reflected as she came out of the cloakroom to find Sylvester waiting for her.

'Come and have a nightcap with me before you go. You've earned it, and I've barely had time to talk to you all evening.'

'Oh, um — well, it is getting late, and . . . ' She glanced at her wristwatch.

It was twelve fifteen.

'Please.'

His gaze gleamed at her, catapulting Kat's pulses, as well as her heartbeat, into hyperdrive. 'I can't. I have to drive, so . . . ' She shrugged.

'Okay, I'll make some more coffee then. Go into the sitting room and I'll be through in a couple of minutes.'

'Joan has gone to bed,' Kat told him.

He regarded her, his head tilted to one side. 'I know. I can do some things myself,' he quietly said. 'I'm not completely useless.'

Kat bit at her bottom lip. 'S-sorry, I didn't mean . . . ' She felt the warmth of a blush begin to creep up into her face.

Sylvester reached out to her and gently touched her with one hand. The skin of her face flamed hotly. 'I don't know another woman who blushes like you do.'

Kat smiled weakly at him. 'S-sorry.'

'Don't apologise. It's charming,' he murmured.

And naive and utterly juvenile, she mutely contradicted. 'Do you know, I think I will go.' Her heart was leaping in her chest. What the hell was happening here? She took a step back from him. She'd suddenly had the most compelling urge to throw herself into his arms.

'Why?' Eyes the colour of wet slate burned into hers. 'You're not frightened of me, are you?'

'Good heavens, no.' She attempted a cool laugh. It didn't quite come off. In fact, it sounded more like a hysterical squeak. 'It's just — I must go. I-I can't . . . ' Words failed her. Whatever must he be thinking? She was behaving like the schoolgirl he'd known all those years ago.

'Which must mean,' he drawled, 'you're frightened of yourself and what you might do.'

'N-no, I'm not. Whatever do you mean? What I might do?'

This all ensured that she was so distracted with trying to rebut his preposterous remarks that she completely failed to notice he'd moved closer. Suddenly, their faces were only an inch apart.

'I'll make it a little more explicit, shall I? Of what your own emotions might tempt you to do.'

His voice throbbed deep in his throat and his breath feathered the still-flushed skin of her face. She could smell his aftershave; it filled her nostrils and made her head spin crazily. Oh, God . . . She breathed in the man-scent of him. It was seductive and utterly irresistible. He was right — she was frightened of what she might be driven to do if he kissed her. What responses he might induce.

'Qu-quite sure. Look, I must go.'

'And if I say that I don't want you to?'

Totally bereft of words by this time, she couldn't even muster a squeak. She simply gazed up at him, feeling as if she were drowning in the liquid depths of his eyes. She heard his groan quite clearly then. Again, it came from way down in his throat. He slid an arm around her waist, pulling her against him, measuring her curvaceous length along the harder lines of his body. Her lips parted as she stared helplessly up at him. He gave another low groan before cupping the back of her head with his other hand and lowering his mouth towards hers.

The arm that was still around her waist moved lower, and he pressed her harder against him. It was a boldly intimate gesture, and it ensured she felt his arousal. She couldn't move, so overwhelming was the onslaught of longing that engulfed her. She simply waited, breath trapped in her throat, for whatever was about to happen. It didn't take long. He moved his head that last millimetre and, all of a sudden, his mouth was clamped to hers. His kiss was urgent, hungry; utterly demanding. Kat couldn't resist. She parted her lips to him and allowed his tongue to slide inside. It flicked against hers, making her pulses leap and her stomach melt. Her arms slid, of their own volition, up his chest, so that her trembling fingers could entangle themselves in the hair at the nape of his neck.

There was another soft groan. This time it was her, Kat realised. She arched her body, offering herself up to his caress. One hand cupped her breast, gently squeezing, his thumb brushing the peak, the other fondling her hips. Her legs parted beneath the thrust of his thigh as desire flamed deep within her. She pressed herself even closer; so close, she felt as if they were one person and she was dissolving into him.

But then reality stepped in, harsh and uncompromising. This couldn't be happening; it simply couldn't. She couldn't allow it to happen. The words seared themselves into her brain. What was she thinking? This was the man who was most likely responsible for the persecution of her mother. As much as she wanted to believe it wasn't, she couldn't be sure.

She struggled to pull away, lowering her arms and placing both hands, palms flat, against his chest, trying to hold him off. He didn't release her at first, pulling her inexorably back into him. He opened his eyes and she saw the passion that was still flaming there. Oh good Lord, he wasn't about to let her go.

But she was wrong. The second he saw her expression, he released her. 'What's wrong?' he huskily demanded.

'This is,' she lamely said.

'Why?' She saw the frustration flare upon his face, and he reached for her again. 'We were both enjoying it.'

She evaded his grasp. 'No, I can't — wasn't — '

'Liar,' he groaned. 'Kat, you can't leave me like this. Look at me. I want you. I always wanted you, even as a boy at school.'

'Really!' She gave a brittle laugh. 'I find that extremely hard to believe. I heard you — when a friend asked you if you saw something you liked when you were looking at me, you-you said, 'Are you kidding? I like my girls a bit more' — now what was it? Oh yes, 'a bit more mature and with a bit of glamour.' Do you know how that made me feel? What it did to my self-esteem? Which, at the age of fourteen, wasn't great.'

He widened his eyes at her. 'Did I say that?'

'Yes, you did.'

'Christ, Kat, I was a boy. If I did indeed say that, it was probably because I felt embarrassed that someone had seen me looking. I apologise.'

'Mind you,' she went on as if he hadn't spoken, 'in a way I suppose it worked for me. Because after that I made more of an effort. It helped me make the most of myself; made me determined, in fact, to prove you wrong. So I should really be thanking you. You could well have been the one to make me what I am now.'

'I can't honestly say I recall any of it.'

'No,' she witheringly said, 'I don't suppose you do. Anyway, our relationship — if you can call it that — is a purely professional one, and that's the way I intend to keep it. So now that that's clear, I have to go. My mother will be wondering — '

'Your mother?' He snorted. 'Good God, Kat, you're a grown woman, not a girl anymore.'

'And certainly not the impressionable girl I was in our schooldays,' she bit out. 'I'm leaving. I don't need this type of harassment.'

His good-looking features darkened, almost menacingly. Kat flinched. She knew nothing about this man; didn't know what he would be capable of if really provoked.

'Harassment? What the hell are you talking about? You were as keen for that lovemaking as I was, so don't give me that rubbish. Harassment, indeed. Think about it. I'm a man, you're a woman.' He slowly enunciated the words, as if she were still a child and therefore might have trouble understanding him. Her hackles rose against what she interpreted as blatant condescension. 'We're built for making love. It's a perfectly natural thing to do.'

'For you, maybe. Not for me.'

'Why not? Is there something wrong with you? You're not frigid, that was more than obvious. You responded fully. In fact, I'd have said you couldn't get enough. Was that what you were frightened of?' His mouth twisted in a sneer. 'That you'd actually show some real emotion, some passion?'

She glowered at him. 'I wasn't frightened.'

'Liar,' he softly murmured.

She ignored that and said, 'And now I've had more than enough. I'll see myself out.'

And that was exactly what she did.

* ★ ★

It was well past one o'clock in the morning by the time Kat reached her mother's flat. She saw at once that all the lights were blazing. Something was wrong. She quickly let herself into the shop and headed for the stairs that led up to the living quarters. She leaped up them, calling as she went, 'Mum? Mum? Are you okay?'

Ruth came to the top of the stairs, her face the colour of skimmed milk. 'Oh, thank heavens, you're back.' Her eyes glistened with incipient tears. Even as she spoke, the landline phone rang. 'Oh, not again,' she moaned.

'Who is it?' Kat gasped. 'What's wrong?'

'Y-you answer it, please.'

Kat lifted the receiver to her ear. 'Hello, Kat Lucas speaking.' There was no answer, just the sound of someone breathing heavily, and then an echoing silence. 'Hello, who is this? Who's there?' But it was evident the other party had ended the call. She replaced the receiver and swung back to her mother. 'What's going on?'

'It's been like that all evening — well,

since ten thirty. Every half hour, on the dot. I almost called you, but I thought you'd be busy and well, what could you have done?'

Kat lifted the receiver again and dialled 1471, only to be told by the automated voice that the caller had withheld the number. But then she'd expected that. 'Did whoever it was say anything at all?'

'No, just the sound of someone breathing. It's him, isn't it? Sylvester Jordan.'

Kat frowned. She'd have to come clean now. Despite their heated exchange just moments ago, she couldn't allow Sylvester to be blamed when she knew all too well it couldn't possibly have been him. She took a deep breath and began to speak. 'I don't see how it could have been him. I've been in the same room as him all evening, right up until ten minutes ago.'

Ruth stared at her, her expression one of utter disbelief. 'You've what?

You've been with him? I knew you were up to something,' she burst out, 'when you avoided answering some of my questions about seeing him and his assistant. You could barely look me in the eye. How could you, Kat?'

'I catered a dinner party for him, that's all. It's hardly a hanging offence. I need the work, Mum.'

'Even so. To go and work for-for — *that man* . . . ' She spat the last two words out.

'He made no calls, Mum.' But, she belatedly asked herself, could she be one hundred percent sure of that? She'd made several visits to the kitchen, and Sylvester himself had left the room a couple of times — to visit the loo, she'd supposed. He could easily have made the calls then. But no, that didn't work. They'd been made at half-hour intervals since ten thirty, and he certainly hadn't left the room that often. Though she supposed he could have got someone else to do it on his behalf.

'Then he got someone else to do it for him,' Ruth echoed Kat's thoughts precisely. 'Who else could it be but him? Who'd have reason to frighten me like this? And *you've been cooking for him*.' She couldn't have made her disgust any plainer, or her bitter disappointment — which would only deepen if she knew Kat had actually sat at his table with him.

Kat didn't know what to say. Ruth was right. Who else had a motive? No one that she could think of. But then something very disturbing occurred to her. Something that inspired a feeling of utter dismay. Had Sylvester made love to her not out of uncontrollable passion or desire as she'd believed, or he'd given her to believe, but in the hope that if he convinced her he was in love with her and made her fall in love with him, she'd persuade her mother into acquiescence? If he won Kat over, then there was a very good chance that Ruth would follow — and then Charlie too might abandon the fight.

It all sounded horribly plausible. And if she were right — ? Dear God. She drew a shuddering sigh. If she were right, how could she have been so easily taken in?

8

A week later, Sylvester rang Kat and invited her and her mother to dinner at Linford Manor. 'I'm going to ask Charlie Turnbull too. I think it's time we had a real discussion about things, face to face, and tried to hammer out some sort of acceptable deal.' His voice was smooth, his tone suggesting that he had no doubt a deal could be successfully brokered; a deal that would favour him and his plans. Kat could only suppose that, in the event of her failure to fall for his calculating and cold-hearted scheming, he had decided to directly approach Ruth and Charlie. Impress them with his house, his wealth — intimidate them, in other words.

'When?' Kat abruptly asked, irritated by the mere sound of such unassailable confidence in his own ability to gain that which he wanted: a sell-out by the remaining two occupants in the block of shops. Well, her mother would very quickly put him right on that score. In which case, might he reconsider his plans for demolition? Though even Kat had to admit that he'd progressed pretty far along the road to back down now. Still, it was something to hope for. A possibility, at any rate, that made it worth accepting his invitation.

'Tomorrow — seven thirty?'

'Fine.' She hung up. After the manner in which they'd parted the last time, she really didn't know what else to do. Polite conversation was out of the question. And just the sound of his voice was sufficient to shake her equilibrium; that and his insufferable self-possession. Once again, her face burned hotly at the memory of how passionately she'd responded to his lovemaking. How could she have been such a fool? And a gullible fool at that. She didn't know why she was still letting him get to her; he'd probably forgotten all about their kisses. His unmistakable composure told her, more than anything else could have, that they'd meant nothing more to him than some sort of casual dalliance. A dalliance primarily aimed, she was increasingly positive, at convincing her to persuade her mother to sell Petals. In the aftermath of which he would almost certainly be gambling on Charlie also falling into line.

Well, she'd had more than enough of that sort of contemptible behaviour in her marriage. She certainly wasn't going to open herself up to it again, and certainly not with Sylvester Jordan.

But something belatedly occurred to her then. She'd accepted his invitation without giving a thought to how her mother would react to it. Badly, she suspected. In fact, a downright refusal to go couldn't be ruled out, and Kat didn't look forward to having to ring Sylvester and tell him his invitation had been turned down.

* * *

But Ruth surprised her. 'That's fine,' she calmly said when Kat repeated Sylvester's invitation. 'I've got a few things I'd take great pleasure in saying to your precious Mr Jordan.'

Kat's heart immediately went into a nosedive. She could already picture it. Ruth would say exactly what she thought, and nothing — and no one — would stop her. The prospect of that was all it took to instil deep misgiving in Kat, if not fear.

'He's not *my* Mr Jordan, precious or otherwise. He was a client, that's all. It was an evening's work that I couldn't afford to turn down.'

Ruth guffawed her contempt for that. 'Evidently, despite the fact that he's most likely the one persecuting your mother for his own greedy ends. Do you know, I'd rather go broke than do anything for such a man.'

Kat decided not to pour oil on the already heated situation and argue, so instead she meekly said, 'Charlie's going to be there too.'

'Well, that's something. At least we've got reinforcements.' And she guffawed again. She was making it sound as if an entire regiment of people was going to be present, instead of just three of them. Kat knew she had to somehow try and calm her mother down before they turned up at Linford Manor the following evening, otherwise who knew what sort of mayhem would ensue.

'Mum,' she began, 'you will be careful about what you say to him, won't you? I would imagine his tolerance for plain speaking would have a pretty low threshold.'

'Of course I will.' She stared defiantly at Kat. 'Have you ever known me to be rude?'

Kat was lost for words at that. What she considered to be rude and what Ruth considered to be rude were two diametrically opposed things. Ruth called it being honest and straightforward, while most other people deemed it unpleasantly offensive.

She decided to go and have a word

with Charlie and enlist his aid in checking, or trying to at any rate, any sort of impulsive accusations from her mother. Though who was to say that he wouldn't share Ruth's determination to embark upon some plain talking? Still, Kat had to try.

The elderly man was sweeping the floor of his small store. He turned at her entrance and smiled. 'Hello, Kat, love. How're you doing?'

'Fine. Um — has Sylvester Jordan been in touch with you?'

'Yes.' He stopped sweeping and rested an elbow on the top of the broom handle. 'To say I was surprised would be an understatement. Still, if meeting him helps to resolve the impasse we seem to be at, then that can only be a good thing. He said you and Ruth are going too.'

Kat nodded. Charlie was clearly seeing the invitation as something to be welcomed. Maybe he would persuade Ruth to view it in the same way, and everything would be all right, after all.

'Yes.' She studied him for a moment. 'You sound as if you want the whole business settled.'

'I do, yes. I'm too old for all this resistance. I know I haven't been targeted so far, not like your mum has, but . . . well, I don't want to give in and abandon her. She'd be left here on her own, and I can't have that. And we can't be sure that it's Jordan behind the attacks, and not just some local vandal out for a bit of sport, can we?'

Kat eyed him. 'You want to accept the offer to buy, don't you?'

Charlie shrugged his thin shoulders. 'I can't see us winning this particular battle. Jordan's too powerful. Even if it isn't him behind the vandalism, he'll find some other way to get us to leave. But please, don't tell Ruth I've said this. She'd tell me to do what I want, and I just can't.' He sighed. 'I can't leave her.'

Kat didn't say anything, but something struck her as it had once or twice before. As Charlie had said, it was only

Ruth's shop being attacked; he'd been left alone. Which, belatedly, did seem suspicious. Why would Charlie's be left alone when Ruth's was the target of such vandalism? Not only that, but there were also the phone calls to be taken into consideration. She didn't want to think it, but could it be the old man behind everything? He was right there on site, so to speak. He could well be taking note of when Ruth stayed at home, which, if he wished to instil fear into her, would be the ideal time to play the role of vandal, as well as make the anonymous calls. In fact, the more Kat considered it, the more plausible the whole thing became. As Paul had suggested, if the perpetrator — i.e. Charlie — could frighten Ruth into moving out, then he could honourably concede defeat and go too. Yet she couldn't help thinking that if he was so fond of her mother, would he really want to cause her so much distress? So much alarm?

No, she couldn't believe it; refused to

believe it. She'd known Charlie for years. He'd always lived in the town, and had owned his shop for the last twenty years, as he was fond of telling people. He was an integral part of Paradise Road.

However, upon her return to Petals, Kat couldn't resist saying to Ruth, 'I've been wondering — you don't think it could be Charlie behind everything that's been happening, do you? His shop hasn't been attacked, and as far as we know, he's had no anonymous calls either.' Why hadn't one of them thought to ask him? she belatedly wondered. Why hadn't she? She'd just been with him, after all. 'Maybe he wants to accept the offer, and this is his method of — '

Ruth didn't let her finish. 'Don't be ridiculous. Of course it's not Charlie. He'd never do such terrible things. Why would he? He's been just as determined as me not to give way.'

★　★　★

From then on, and despite whatever she did to try and distract herself, Kat found herself viewing the prospect of dinner at Linford Manor with increasing dread, as well as living in fear of whatever it was Ruth was so keen to say to their host — especially now in the light of Kat having catered for him. She knew only too well that if her mother was set upon a certain course of action, practically nothing would deflect her. She tried, without being too obvious, to question Ruth about her intentions, but her diplomacy got her nowhere. A stone sphinx would reveal more of its plans than her mother. Kat just hoped that whatever course she decided on, it wouldn't be serious enough to inspire Sylvester to take any sort of legal action against her.

All of which ensured that by the time seven o'clock arrived — the time Kat had agreed to drive round to collect her mother and Charlie — she was a bundle of jangling nerves. Her apprehension was such that it had even affected her decision about what to wear. Eventually, after practically emptying her entire wardrobe onto the bed, she'd settled on a pair of plain black trousers and an equally plain cream blouse. It concealed her curves very effectively, with its high neck and long sleeves. She didn't want there to be any suggestion of seductiveness. The last thing she wanted was to appear to be inviting any sort of romantic overtures from her host.

Ruth, on the other hand, had done her utmost to look her best. Her choice of a black, slightly glittery dress was, in Kat's opinion, way over the top for what could only be described as a business dinner. Charlie was also smartly attired in a tailored jacket and trousers, complete with silk tie. Kat didn't think she'd ever seen the old man dressed in such a fashion; hadn't thought he possessed a tailored jacket, in fact. She was accustomed to seeing him in jeans and a casual shirt.

The two older people were enjoying a

gin and tonic. Ruth eyed her daughter critically. 'Don't you think you're a little underdressed for dinner at the local manor house? I'm sure Sylvester Jordan is accustomed to his guests being attired in the very latest fashions.'

'It's only a business meal.'

Ruth sniffed her disapproval but said nothing more. It was Charlie who smiled and said, 'I think you look very nice, Kat.'

'Thank you, Charlie. The same goes for you.'

The three of them eventually piled into Ruth's car, as Kat's van wouldn't have been at all suitable to arrive in at the stately portals of Linford Manor, according to the Gospel of Ruth. She'd even insisted on driving. 'I have every intention of drinking water only. I need to keep my wits about me.'

Keep her wits about her? Kat mentally echoed, trying at the same time to halt the downward spiral of her spirits as she anticipated the forthcoming evening and its possible pitfalls.

What did Ruth think Sylvester was going to do or say? Subject her to some sort of inquisition? Waterboard her? Put her on the rack? Mind you, knowing Sylvester as she was coming to, it wouldn't be beyond the realms of likelihood.

Once they arrived at Linford Manor and parked in front of the house, Ruth peered through the windscreen and hissed, 'My God. I'd heard he was rich, but by the looks of this he's a multi-millionaire.' She then eyed her daughter accusingly. 'But of course, you'd know. You've been before. Why didn't you didn't tell me how grand it is?'

'I assumed you'd know, living in the town.'

'Well, I would if it could be seen from the road.'

Oh God, was all Kat could think. It had begun. The evening was going to be a nightmare, she just knew it. For two pins she'd turn round and return home, leaving Ruth and Charlie to it. But of course she didn't. She'd have to see it through and just hope that Ruth wasn't too forthright.

The front door opened and Sylvester himself stood there. He must have heard them arrive. He looked down at the three of them, dithering at the bottom of the steps that led up to the door. His glance skimmed over them, finally coming to rest on Kat. She couldn't help but see the gleam of amusement as he took in the sight of her modest outfit. However, he made no comment. Instead he said, 'Please, come in.'

In single file they trooped up the steps and entered the house. Sylvester took their jackets and disappeared into the cloakroom with them. Ruth's eyes swiftly moved around the huge hallway, but she made no comment, not even a whispered one. Which was just as well, because Sylvester was back almost at once.

So far, save for his own welcoming words, no one had said anything, and the silence was beginning to feel awkward. In an attempt to lighten things, Kat asked, 'No Joan this evening then?'

'No.' Sylvester's gaze fixed upon her, the gleam of suppressed amusement still present. 'It's her night off.' He did smile then. 'But don't worry, she's left us plenty of food. It won't be up to your high standards, of course, but it will be perfectly edible.' He indicated the door leading into the sitting room. 'Please, won't you come in?'

They followed him into the room that Kat remembered from her first visit. To her surprise, there were three other people already there, all with glasses in their hands.

'Let me introduce everyone,' Sylvester said. 'My mother, Maria; my father, Oscar; and, of course my partner, Brett Sinclair.'

So he'd brought in reinforcements, had he? Kat mused. She smiled weakly in Maria's direction. 'We've already met. Hello.'

Maria twitched her lips in what Kat presumed was her rather pathetic attempt at a smile.

Ignoring Kat's murmured remark, Sylvester continued, 'This is Kat; her mother, Ruth; and Charlie Turnbull, Ruth's neighbour. Please, sit down.' He gestured towards the remaining empty seats. Kat chose the armchair furthest away from where she guessed Sylvester would sit. She didn't want to risk the possibility of his proximity weakening her resolve to back her mother and Charlie in the matter of keeping their shops. Not that she intended to say much; she'd leave that to Ruth — unless Ruth got carried away and began to say things she shouldn't. Kat's heart plummeted again at the mere prospect of having to intervene.

'Now, drinks first,' Sylvester was saying, 'then dinner while we discuss the business side of things.'

They emptied their glasses, which in Kat's case — and due solely to her misgivings about the evening in general

— had only taken a moment or two; in fact, she was the first one to set her empty glass on the table that had been placed strategically between them all for that very purpose. Then they all got to their feet. Kat had seen Sylvester's eyebrow go up at the speed with which she'd finished her drink, but in a second uncharacteristic display of sensitivity and tact he refrained from making any sort of comment. Instead, he led them all into the dining room.

The table was plainly laid this time with a simple arrangement of white chrysanthemums in a large porcelain bowl sitting in the centre. There were several tureens of food on hot plates on a side table ready to help themselves from, Kat assumed. Sylvester was obviously keen to emphasise the business aspect of the evening.

The talk was pretty general to begin with. Ruth, to Kat's heartfelt relief, responded to questions and comments politely, with no trace of the belligerence she usually displayed at any mention of their host. In fact, they were on their desserts before Maria broached the subject of Ruth and Charlie moving out, which surprised Kat. She'd expected it to be either Sylvester or Brett who did so.

'I hope you've both considered Sylvester's extremely generous compensation offer,' Maria said, 'because I think it should be stressed that your intransigence is holding everything up.'

'Mother,' Sylvester sharply cut her off, 'I'd prefer it if you left this to me.'

Kat found herself wondering why Maria and Oscar were there in the first place, if they weren't to be allowed a part in the discussion. Sylvester must have invited them. For the first time she wondered if Oscar Jordan had some sort of financial interest in his son's business, so was as keen as Sylvester to get on with the work. Yet so far he'd made little or no contribution to the conversation. Maybe he'd only come along at Maria's insistence. She did seem a forceful woman who delighted in interfering in someone else's business; hence her turning up at Petals. Sylvester had been quite explicit to Kat: it hadn't been at his behest.

Ruth, however, much to Kat's astonishment, replied to Maria with absolute calm and composure. 'We certainly have considered the offer very carefully. But what neither you nor your son seem to have considered is that it is our homes we're talking about, not just our livelihoods. Speaking on my own behalf, I know everyone in the locality, and they know me. They buy all their flowers from me — for weddings, funerals, every important occasion in fact. They trust me to do my best for them, as they do Charlie. We don't see why we should be forced to leave and move to an area where no one will be aware of my reputation, in particular for — well . . . ' She gave a modest smile. ' . . . floral perfection.'

'You're not being forced,' Maria snapped.

'What would you describe it as then?'

Ruth spoke once again with perfect calm, much to Kat's surprise. She'd been expecting a full-blown row to have erupted by this time. They had already been there for a couple of hours.

'Please, Mother,' Sylvester gently rebuked. He then smiled at Ruth, his charm and good looks on full display. 'Ruth — if I may call you that?'

Ruth nodded. 'Of course.' Then, amazingly, she smiled warmly back at him. Kat could only stare in bemusement. Who would have believed it? After all she'd said about Sylvester, Ruth was no more immune to the attractions of a handsome man, even one many years younger, than her daughter was.

'Nobody is forcing you anywhere. Not you — and not you, Mr Turnbull.'

'Call me Charlie,' Charlie good-naturedly put in.

'Thank you, Charlie. I'm prepared to up our offer to — ' And he named a figure that was a full fifty percent more than the original offer.

Kat's eyes widened, as did Charlie's. Her mother would be crazy not to accept. She could buy a bigger shop in a more affluent area, as could Charlie. Charlie's eyes were shining as he said, 'Well, I for one — '

Ruth cut him off. 'The answer's still no, I'm afraid, Mr Jordan. No amount of money will convince me that moving is the right thing to do, not at my time of life, and not at any price.'

Kat gazed quizzically at her mother. She was making it sound as if she was the wrong side of seventy, instead of the mere fifty-six that she was.

'Mr Turnbull?' Sylvester turned to the older man. 'You wanted to say something?'

Charlie didn't at first respond to this question, even though it was directed solely at him. Instead, he gazed almost beseechingly at Ruth. Ruth smartly shook her head at him.

'I'm with Ruth,' he finally and quietly said.

Kat thought it was time she spoke up.

She could see that Charlie wanted to accept. 'Mum, I really think you should — '

'I've made up my mind, Kat, as has Charlie.'

Kat fell silent. Her mother was adamant. No reasoned argument was going to change her mind — as she well knew from past experience. She glanced at Sylvester. He was looking at Brett. His mouth was compressed into a thin line. He nodded at the other man.

Brett began to speak. Like Oscar Jordan, he'd contributed little to the evening's conversation other than the most commonplace remarks. 'You're standing in the way of a development that will bring new life to this area, which is dying on its feet. There are hardly any shops left. How much longer do you think you can continue? The customers you're so keen to keep will start going elsewhere — somewhere where there are more shops, more amenities to choose from. They may even move away, and then where will you be? Bankrupt, I shouldn't wonder.' He regarded Ruth intently and through narrowed eyes.

But Ruth, refusing to back down and defiant to the last, stared straight back at him. 'The answer is still no. I'm staying. Charlie must do what he wants, what he thinks best, but I'm not going anywhere. And, you know, I have faith; faith enough in my customers to be sure that they won't desert me.'

'Well,' Brett snapped, 'let's hope you're right.'

Charlie stared helplessly at Ruth for a long moment but then murmured, 'I'll stay too.'

'So with that, our business is concluded. Thank you for a nice meal, Mr Jordan,' Ruth said, 'but I think it's time we left. Kat, Charlie — ?' With utter confidence that her two companions would obediently follow suit, she got to her feet.

Brett also stood. 'Okay, you win, we'll add another twenty thousand to the offer — for each of you. Not even you two can refuse that.'

'Oh, but we can, Mr Sinclair, we most certainly can,' Ruth declared in her no-arguments-will-be-tolerated tone. It was one that Kat recalled only too well from her youth, and one that she'd never quite got up the courage to dispute. She smiled to herself. It had certainly silenced Brett Sinclair — momentarily, at any rate. 'And let me just add, if we — I — get any more persecution, threats, or silent phone calls, I'll be contacting the police and voicing my suspicions as to who is behind it all.'

'You can call who you want,' Brett retaliated, swiftly rediscovering his powers of speech. 'And, if I might be permitted to ask, what proof do you have that we're behind it? I presume that's what you're suggesting. The truth is, you have none.' His smile was a confident one. 'Because none of it is down to us. That's not our way of doing things.'

It was now Maria's turn to get to her feet. 'Oscar,' she cried, 'do something.'

'Like what?' her husband said. 'It's best to leave it to Sylvester.'

'Oh, is that so?' Ruth blurted. 'In which case, why exactly are you here? To outnumber us, to provide a bit more intimidation?'

'Certainly not,' Maria bit back. 'We're here simply to support our son.' She totally ignored her husband's cautionary, 'Maria, stay out of it,' reinforcing Kat's theory that she was the driving force in that marriage. She must be the one who'd influenced Sylvester the most. Kat nibbled at her lip. She should have known it was going too well. Was it all about to kick off? Should she intervene?

Before she could do so, however, Ruth retorted, 'Well, I have to say, your son seems to have done very well so far in his efforts to make us leave — without your support.'

Kat stared at her mother in horror. She'd gone too far, just as she invariably did. She then had to watch as Sylvester's expression darkened and his jaw line hardened implacably. It was something she'd seen several times before, and it was something that warned of serious danger if matters progressed any further.

His voice, when he finally spoke, reinforced that impression; it was glacial and low. And it had far more impact than any amount of shouting would have done. 'I have done nothing so far other than to offer you enough money to start a new life in a more prosperous area. So I should be very careful about what insinuations you make, or it'll be me calling the police, I can guarantee that.'

Ruth's expression of determination wavered as she slowly comprehended that she was standing on very shaky ground indeed. Brett Sinclair was right, Kat conceded. Her mother had no proof it was them behind things.

However, Ruth wasn't one to demonstrate any sign of weakness, and she swiftly recovered herself enough to command, 'Come on, Kat, Charlie.'

Then she turned and strode from the room, head defiantly in the air, leaving Kat and Charlie with no option but to follow her.

Later that night, someone heaved several bricks through both shop windows, completely shattering the glass in each, which did seem to blow a massive hole in Kat's theory that Charlie could be behind everything.

Once again, suspicion rested squarely upon Sylvester.

9

Then, just when Kat thought things could get no worse, they did. A zillion times worse.

Max, her ex-husband, returned to Market Linford.

It was Daisy who broke the news. They'd met for a drink at their customary haunt, the Green Frog. 'I've got something to tell you, Kat,' she said eventually, and with more than a little apprehension. 'I can only assume you haven't heard or you'd surely have mentioned it by now. You're not going to like it.' She pulled a face.

Kat stared at her. Oh God, what now? As if things weren't bad enough already. 'What? What is it?' It couldn't be something else to do with Sylvester, could it?

'Max has come back,' Daisy blurted. 'Even got his old job back.'

'You're kidding.'

'No, I'm not. I wouldn't kid about something like that.' She was patently offended by the fact that her best friend thought she'd play such a cruel trick on her. 'He hasn't been in touch then?'

'No, he hasn't, and he'd better not either.' Kat took a large gulp of her wine, and then without thinking took another. 'He'll get very short shrift, I can . . . ' Her gaze reached over Daisy's shoulder and her words petered out. 'Oh no,' she murmured.

'What?' Daisy turned to look as well. 'Oh, good Lord.'

Max had just walked in — alone. Kat's first thought was, where was the woman he'd left town with? The woman he'd betrayed her with?

He glanced around the room and saw Kat and Daisy; then without as much as breaking his stride, he crossed the room towards them. Nothing had changed, Kat mused. Still the same arrogant Max, sure of his welcome anywhere, no matter what transgressions he'd been guilty of. What was it with men today? she wondered. Sylvester was the same. Supremely confident of his own worth; positive that, no matter whom it inconvenienced, whatever he wanted he should have — without argument or controversy. It was infuriating.

'I thought I might find you two in here.' He smiled breezily at Kat, for all the world as if nothing had ever gone wrong between the two of them.

Kat gritted her teeth. 'What do you want?' she bit out.

'You,' he softly murmured.

'Huh!' Kat burst out, causing the heads of several people to turn. He grinned. 'Huh!' she snorted for a second time.

'Kat,' Daisy hissed, 'you're beginning to sound like an athlete on steroids.'

Kat stared at her for a minute, then hissed back, 'An athlete on steroids? How the hell do you know what an athlete on steroids sounds like?'

'I don't. I just thought of it to shut you up.'

Throughout all of this, Matt grinned, albeit slightly fixedly as he cast a nervous glance round the room. They were the focus of everyone's attention by this time.

Kat turned her gaze back to him and said, 'You certainly didn't want me — ooh, now when was it? — oh yes, five years ago. You left me for — who was it?' She cast her gaze upwards as if deep in thought. 'Ah yes, Toni.'

'I didn't leave you. You kicked me out,' he sharply riposted; he was clearly annoyed at her display of irony.

'So I did. I wonder why?' Again, she seemed to be giving the question a great deal of thought.

Max, for his part, was looking more and more embarrassed. He'd realised they were still the object of everyone's attention. He lowered his voice. 'Look, I know I behaved badly, but — '

'And where is the delectable and utterly irresistible Toni?' Kat made a great show of glancing around the bar, slowly taking in every inch and not appearing to notice the interest of all the other people who were there. Eventually she glanced back at Max and said, 'I don't see her. Did you cheat on her, too? What is it they say — ? Oh yes, once a cheat, always a cheat.'

'Kat,' Daisy once again hissed in her ear, 'keep it down, for God's sake. Sylvester Jordan's just walked in. Do you want him to hear everything?'

'Oh, good grief,' Kat moaned, 'the evening just gets better and better.'

'Who's Sylvester Jordan?' Max asked, not bothering to hide the relief he felt to have the heat removed from him, for the moment at least. He glanced across the bar towards Sylvester. 'Is that him? I don't think I know him.'

'Where is the delectable Toni?' Kat asked for a second time. She wasn't about to be sidetracked with questions about Sylvester. In fact, Sylvester was the very last person she wished to talk about.

'Haven't a clue.' His confidence seemingly restored, Max airily said, 'We

189

parted ways a while back.'

'Oh no,' Kat cried with much exaggerated and extremely mocking sympathy, 'she didn't kick you out too, did she? Wise woman.'

'No,' Max bit back. 'I left of my own accord. Look, do you mind if I sit down?'

'Yes, I do, actually. I don't drink with reptiles.'

Max gave a shout of laughter. 'The same old Kat. Still not pulling any punches.' He regarded her from beneath lowered lashes but made no attempt to sit down. 'Who are you seeing nowadays?'

'No one. I'm far too busy building up my business.'

'Yes, I heard you'd got a catering set-up going. Doing well, is it?'

'Fantastically.' She sensed Daisy's wry sideways glance, rather than saw it.

'Do you know, Kat, I'm not surprised you're still single,' he blurted. 'You always were a bit on the hard side, not inclined to suffer fools.'

'How right you are — and you were the biggest fool of all.' She took another mouthful — or three — of her wine, ignoring Daisy's muted, 'Kat, slow down.'

'Yet, I suffered you for three years, didn't I?' she hissed. 'Still, that showed me. Taught me a very valuable lesson, one which I have kept in mind ever since.'

'Kat,' Daisy tried again to calm things down. 'Most of the pub can hear you.'

'Everything all right here?'

Kat looked up and found herself looking at Sylvester. He stood to one side of Max.

'Well,' Kat whooped, 'whaddyaknow, another reptile has joined us.'

Daisy elbowed her hard in her side.

'Ouch,' Kat grumbled. 'What did you do that for?' She glowered at her friend.

Sylvester's eyes narrowed as he said, 'Won't you introduce me, Kat?'

'Sylvester Jordan, meet Max Bellini, my ex-husband and ex-local lothario.'

Neither man spoke, although they did exchange lengthy glances.

'This, Max,' Kat went on, more than a little tipsily now, and with much arm waving, 'is the man who-who's determined to force my mother, a helpless old woman, out of her home and business, in order to erect a-a department store. Can you — can you believe that? It will destroy Paradise Road — destroy the community.'

'Helpless old woman?' Sylvester chuckled with amusement. 'I don't think your mother would appreciate that description.'

'Neither do I,' Daisy softly put in.

'She struck me as a very spirited and determined woman,' Sylvester finished. 'And I'm not trying to force anyone out of anywhere, let a lone destroy Paradise Road and its community. That's if you can describe the two remaining shops and a handful of somewhat rundown houses as a community.'

'Then how would you describe bricks heaved through windows — Mum's and

Charlie's — the night we came to yours; anonymous phone calls; lit fireworks and manure pushed through the letterbox? Gentle persuasion?' She waved her arm even more energetically, knocking over her wine glass in the process and splashing Daisy with red wine.

'Kat,' Daisy exclaimed, 'watch it!'

Sylvester didn't seem to have noticed her clumsiness. 'I've made them an extremely good offer.'

'Yes, after you'd failed with all the other things I-I've mentioned.'

He was starting to look angry now; the skin of his face had paled and his eyes darkened dramatically. 'I have never, ever tried to scare or intimidate anyone. How many times do I have to say it?'

Max was looking on in bewilderment. 'What the hell's been going on?'

'Ask Mr Jordan,' Kat ground out.

'I think you'd better go, Jordan,' Max put in then.

'What an excellent idea,' Kat said.

'And why don't you go with him, Max? I'd like to enjoy my wine.'

'What's left of it,' Daisy muttered at her side. 'Most of it's on my jeans.'

Kat stared at her empty glass in amazement. 'Where's that gone?' All of a sudden, she became aware of her head spinning and her stomach churning. She tried to stand up. 'Daisy, I think I'll go home — I've had no dinner.' But all she did was topple back onto her seat.

Max chuckled. 'Had a bit too much, have we?'

'Oh, shut up,' Kat irritably told him.

'I will,' he amicably agreed. 'I've got to go see someone, anyway.'

'Sure you have. What's her name?' Kat slurred.

'It's not her, it's him,' Max told her with a smug smile. 'And his name is Jack — if you're interested.'

'Take it from me, I'm not.'

Kat's head was all over the place. She needed to get home, and quickly. Her home, not her mother's. Ruth would have too much to say about her state of intoxication. It would be just one more blot on her already stained copybook, because if there was one thing her mother hated, it was drunkenness. Something she'd seen a bit too often in her late husband's final years.

Max left, thankfully; irritatingly, Sylvester stayed. He was watching her now, a frown of concern tugging at his brow.

'You can go, too,' she airily told him, waving him away. 'God, some people simply can't take a hint. Daisy, tell him.'

'Come on,' Daisy said. 'I'll get you home.'

'Do you have a car?' Sylvester softly asked.

'No, we walked here.' Daisy now also frowned as she assessed the condition of her friend. 'And, frankly, I don't know if she'll be up to it.'

'Don't worry. I'll take her.'

'Daisy, you come with me — please. Back to my place, not Mum's,' Kat mumbled.

'Okay. Where does she live?' Sylvester asked.

'Number twenty-eight Maple Road. The upstairs flat, twenty-eight A. Do you want me to come with you?'

'No, I'm sure I'll be able to manage.'

'Okay. I'll ring Ruth and let her know what's happening, so she doesn't worry when Kat doesn't arrive back.'

As for Kat, she didn't say anything. Belatedly, she didn't care who took her home as long as someone did. She'd have gone with the devil himself if he'd offered to drive her. Mind you, she thought with amusement, she supposed that was what she was doing.

Sylvester led her from the pub to his car, which fortunately was parked immediately opposite. He opened the front passenger door and practically lifted her in.

'Th-thank you.' Her head banged hard against the head rest as her eyes closed. 'I'm sorry. I'm not much of a-a drinker.'

'I can see that,' Sylvester gently said. 'How much have you had?'

'Too much. I thought it would act as an anaesthetic, which I suppose it has.'

He grinned and walked round the vehicle to climb in on the driver's side and start the engine. It took only minutes to reach Maple Road, whereupon Sylvester helped her out of the car and through the door that opened onto the flight of stairs that led up to the first-floor apartments.

Once they had struggled to the top — he once again had to practically carry her — he asked, 'Got your key?'

'My key? Oh no,' she groaned. 'I've left it at Mum's. I was originally intending to go back there. Oh God.'

'Don't worry, I'll take you there.'

'No, no, please don't. She mustn't see me like this. Oh, good grief, what have I done?'

'Okay.' Sylvester drawled the single word. 'Well, as I see it, there's only one thing to do.'

'What?' A sense of impending doom was beginning to filter through her feeling of intoxication.

'You'll have to come home with me.'

10

Realising Sylvester's arm was still around her waist, Kat quickly yanked herself away, only to instantly lose her balance and stagger backwards, forcing him to make a grab for her once more.

She glared up at him, stiff with indignation, and said, 'I'm not going home with you.' Once again she tried to free herself, batting at him with her hands. 'I'm no-not that sort of girl. Woman.'

'I know you're not.' Sylvester's voice quivered as he struggled against his laughter, at the same time managing to hold her on to her as well as keep her upright. 'You made that very clear the night of my dinner party, as I recall.'

'That's all right then.'

'So is that settled? We've agreed you're not that kind of woman.' Again his voice quivered. 'But you'll come home with me anyway?'

As intoxicated as Kat was, she could see the sense in what he was suggesting. She peered up at him. 'Separate bedrooms?'

'Separate bedrooms,' he readily agreed.

'Okay.'

It didn't take as long to get back down the stairs as it had taken to get up, so they were quickly back in Sylvester's car and on their way to Linford Manor. The house was on the opposite side of town to Kat's flat, and a couple of miles beyond the perimeter, so Sylvester had the time to ask, 'Max is your ex-husband?'

She nodded.

'How long were you married?'

'Th-three years. The biggest mistake of my life,' she muttered. 'It's what turned me into the bitter spinster I now am.'

He slanted an amused glance at her. 'Well, that's not quite the way I'd describe you.'

'How *would* you describe me?' Oh God, intoxication was making her rash. Did she really want to hear the answer?

'Well, let's see.' Taking a leaf out of her book, he made a great show of giving the question thorough consideration before saying, 'You're a feisty modern woman, and a very lovely one at that. You know what you want and you go all out to get it. I admire that.'

A warm sensation began to creep over Kat. 'D-do you?'

'Yes. You've started your own business.'

'You wouldn't be so admiring if you knew the true state of that.'

'Oh?' He slanted another glance at her, a more penetrating one this time. 'What's happened?'

'No more bookings. Not for the foreseeable future, at any rate.'

That blunt statement seemed to surprise him and he didn't immediately respond.

'Not quite the successful business-woman you thought, eh?' she quipped.

'It doesn't change my opinion of you, Kat,' he quietly said. 'It's probably just a blip. I'm sure things will improve.'

'Huh. I wish.'

They finished the journey in silence, mainly because Sylvester seemed very preoccupied.

Kat chewed at her bottom lip. Damn it. She'd said too much; much too much. He was the last person she wanted to know about the financial trouble she was in, mainly because she wasn't sure that he wouldn't try to use it to somehow persuade Ruth to accept his extremely generous offer of compensation — if only to be in a position to help her daughter out. However, she had told him and it was too late now to retract her impetuous words. She was so stupid. For the umpteenth time her tongue had run away with her brain.

But it wasn't until they reached the entrance to his house that the reality of her situation and what she'd agreed to dawned upon Kat. She'd be in his house, alone with him all night — well, apart from his children; they'd be somewhere, she supposed, and of course Joan — but she'd be in her own room. Suppose he tried to make love to her again? He'd agreed to separate bedrooms, but that didn't ensure he'd remain in his own. Could she trust him? And would she have the strength to resist him if he decided to try his luck again? She couldn't deny she was attracted to him, and in her inebriated state . . . well, anything could happen. Her heart lurched as she remembered his kiss. He'd been very good, very practised.

But Kat's fears proved groundless. He was the perfect gentleman. He ushered her into the kitchen, where he made her a hot, strong coffee — he had a whisky — after which he escorted her upstairs to a large and mind-blowingly luxurious bedroom, still holding her by the elbow, as if afraid she might fall. He even pulled out a nightdress from somewhere while she sat on the excessively comfortable four-poster canopied bed, looking around her. She gazed at the light oak furniture, not fitted but all free-standing — the wardrobe large enough to contain every item of clothing she possessed and a lot more besides; the flatscreen television and DVD player; the pair of armchairs in front of it; the rich brocade curtains with so much fabric in them, they finished in extravagant puddles on the carpet.

She sighed. So this was how the wealthy lived and slept. Did he keep a stock of nightdresses, she suddenly wondered, ready for this very eventuality? Knowing him as she was coming to, she wouldn't be surprised.

'The en-suite is through that door.' He pointed to the door on the opposite side of the room to the one they'd come through. 'You'll find towels and all that you'll need for a night's stay.'

'Were you expecting an overnight guest?'

'No, Joan keeps all the guest rooms and their en-suites fully prepared, fortunately.' He smiled at her suddenly. Her heart performed a couple of somersaults and her pulse madly raced. 'Will you be able to manage?' He belatedly looked concerned.

'Oh yes,' she hastily assured him. The last thing she wanted was to have him offering to help her into bed. She couldn't be sure she wouldn't be tempted to accept.

'Right. Only, I could fetch Joan.'

Disappointment surged through her. So he hadn't been offering to assist. Oh, for heaven's sake, what was wrong with her? She couldn't have seriously been contemplating taking him up on any offer he might make, could she? If she were, then she must be considerably more intoxicated than she'd thought.

'I'll leave you to it then. I'll see you in the morning at whatever time suits you. I'll be here all day.'

He stared down at her, his gaze a smouldering one. She couldn't help herself: she tilted her head backwards, arching her throat, and looked up at him. He made a move towards her. Oh God, he was going to kiss her — and the way she was feeling, she knew she wouldn't be able to resist him.

Her breathing quickened as she surrendered to the yearning to feel his arms around her; to feel his lips on hers. Her breasts heaved, her eyes closed, and she fell backwards, her arms moving up above her head to rest flat on the bed. It was a position of blatant submission; invitation, even. She waited, hardly daring to breathe, anticipating his lovemaking. But then, shockingly, his hands fastened onto her arms and he dragged her back up.

'Kat.' The single word was groaned.

'Yes,' she whispered. She opened her eyes to see him leaning into her, his mouth a mere inch from hers. His eyes were almost black. A single muscle flexed in his jaw. 'Sylvester,' she murmured.

'Go to bed.' The words were harsh; guttural. He released her, almost brutally pushing her away from him.

'Before I change my mind.' He then turned and strode to the door.

She stared after him, not believing what had just happened. 'Sylvester — please . . . '

But he didn't answer.

*　*　*

The next morning Kat opened her eyes only to instantly close them again, as she fervently prayed to die right there and then. She moaned, and it wasn't just because of the way her head was hammering. She was at Linford Manor. The memories began to stir. Oh no. She'd been so drunk, Sylvester had had no choice but to bring her here. She groaned and buried her aching head beneath the fluffy pillows, desperately trying to also bury several more disturbing recollections that were gradually beginning to surface.

Tiny snippets revealed themselves to her in slow motion. Max had been in the pub, then Sylvester had come in. To relieve her stress, she'd gulped carelessly at her wine, consuming it much too quickly. She recalled practically shouting at Max; and then there was Sylvester. What had she said to him? She couldn't remember — although she had some sort of dim memory of trying to kiss him.

It all came back in a single, horrifying flash. She'd lain back on the bed, practically offering herself to him. Practically — ? There was no practically about it; and he'd — she wailed out loud — he'd turned her down. How would she be able to ever face him again?

There was a knock on her bedroom door. She sat bolt upright. The room swam sickeningly around her. What if it was him? She must look terrible, and her head was in imminent danger of splitting apart. Frantically, she smoothed her nightdress down, checking it was exactly where it should be. She didn't want to look as if she were trying to proposition him again. She closed her eyes in sheer despair.

'Kat?'

She heaved a huge sigh of relief. It was Joan.

'I've brought you a cup of coffee.'

'Oh, please, come in.'

The door opened and the house-keeper walked in, holding a tray with a cafetiere upon it along with a single cup, a small jug, and a sugar bowl.

'Oh, you're an angel,' Kat breathed. 'Just what I need.'

The older woman smiled at her. 'I've made it good and strong. That'll soon revive you.'

Kat, somewhat uneasily, wondered exactly what Sylvester had told her about the previous evening; how he'd explained Kat's surprising presence in one of his guest bedrooms.

'Mr Sylvester said you were left without a lift home, and you'd also left your door key at your mother's, so he brought you here.'

Kat searched her face for any sign of disapproval, any sign that she knew the true story, but there was nothing. 'Yes, that's right. I didn't want to disturb my mother; she'd have been in bed. Such a stupid thing to do.' She smiled weakly at the housekeeper.

'You don't have to explain anything to me, Kat.' She smiled again. Yet there was a hint of something that told Kat she, at the very least, had some sort of suspicion about the truth of the events of the evening before. 'Um, I hope you won't think me presumptuous, but I've brought these with me.' She held out a box of paracetamol.

'Thank you, Joan. And no, I don't think you're being at all presumptuous.'

As she finished speaking, the sounds of children's' voices reached her from further down the hallway. A woman's voice added itself to the cacophony of shouting and laughing. 'Josh, stop that. You'll hurt Sam.'

Kat glanced up at Joan.

'That's Debbie, the boys' nanny. She lives in, of course, so you'll be seeing her later on. Mr Sylvester couldn't manage without her. Well, I'll leave you in peace. Breakfast is laid in the breakfast room, next door to the kitchen. Whenever you're ready.'

'Right. Thank you.'

'Mr Sylvester is working in his den at the moment, but I'm sure he'll join you.' And she all but winked at Kat.

Kat stared after her. What in heaven's name had Sylvester said to Joan about her? Surely she didn't think there was something of a romantic nature between them? She might do if he'd told her he'd be breakfasting with Kat. She felt her face flame hotly then at the mere prospect of joining him for that meal. It would bestow an unmistakable and unwelcome intimacy upon their relationship, if it could be described as such. And that, viewed in the harsh light of morning, was the last thing Kat wanted. Could she somehow make her escape without having to face that ordeal? But wouldn't that be rude? Sylvester had gone to a lot of trouble for her the evening before. How could she repay that by running out on him, without as much as a thank-you?

Something else occurred to her then: she'd have to lie to her mother. She couldn't possibly tell her where she'd spent the night. Her mother would go ballistic. Kat could already hear her: *So, not content with cooking for him, you've also slept with him. How could you?* Because, despite the separate rooms, that was exactly how Ruth would view it. Of course, she need not mention it at all. But supposing Ruth had rung the flat and there had been no answer? She'd be bound to ask where Kat had been. Should she say she'd stayed at Daisy's? No, that would be involving her friend in a deliberate deception. And she dimly recalled Daisy saying something about ringing Ruth and telling her where Kat would be. Oh, what an unholy mess.

She gulped the coffee down and felt it scalding her tongue and throat. She'd face Ruth's questions, she decided, when and if they arose.

After a long, cool shower, she dressed in the previous day's clothes, pulling a face at having to put the same garments on again. She hadn't even got her make-up with her. She did have some lipstick and a hairbrush in her handbag, but that was all. She muttered a silent prayer to whoever it was who decided these things that Sylvester would be too busy to see her — or, better still, that he would already have left the house, despite saying the night before that he'd be home all day.

But her prayers were ignored. As luck would have it, as she made her way down the last couple of stairs into the hallway, he walked out of what she presumed was his den.

'Ah, there you are,' he greeted her. 'Did you have a good night?'

He gave no indication that he recalled anything of the seductive way she'd behaved towards him the previous night. Nonetheless, and despite her immense relief, all she could muster was a slight nod of the head.

He eyed her more intently then. 'You look a bit wan. Can I get you some aspirin?'

Gee, thanks, she silently retaliated. *You really know how to make a gal feel good.* 'I-I'm fine, thank you.'

'Well, I'm sure some breakfast will put the roses back in your cheeks.' He smiled teasingly.

Oh God, she agonised, he knew exactly how she was feeling. How embarrassing. He'd have her down as a drunk from this time on. But worse than that, there was more than a dawning hint of something in his expression that suggested he remembered all too clearly the events in her bedroom the night before.

'Come along.' He stretched out an arm and ushered her into the breakfast room. 'You can meet my sons. Here they are.' He grinned with undisguised pride.

Kat saw two small boys already sitting at the table, consuming boiled eggs and fingers of toast. The second they spotted their father they both called, 'Daddy, here's Daddy.' The one who looked youngest leaped from his seat and hurled himself at Sylvester, who promptly lifted him up to allow the child to put both arms tightly round his neck.

Kat smiled at the scene unfolding before her. Whatever else Sylvester might be, he was clearly a much-loved father.

'I want you all to meet Kat Lucas. Kat, this little tinker is Samuel.' He pointed to the other slightly older-looking boy standing to one side. 'And that's Joshua.'

Two pairs of eyes, the exact same shade of grey as their father's, settled upon Kat. Samuel, still in his father's arms, beamed in what looked like genuine delight. The older one, Joshua, just stared before saying almost grudgingly, 'Are you Daddy's new friend?'

Not surprisingly, Kat found herself wondering how many other women Sylvester had introduced to his sons.

'Well,' she said with a smile, 'sort of, I suppose.' She slanted a glance at Sylvester. He was making no attempt to hide his amusement at her quandary. For the second time she suspected he knew exactly what she was thinking.

'You'll give Kat the wrong impression, Josh,' he then smoothly said. 'I'm not in the habit of bringing women to breakfast. Kat and I have only just recently met again. We were at school together.'

Kat belatedly became aware of a third pair of eyes appraising her: Debbie the nanny's. And their expression, when she looked, was one of unmistakable hostility. Kat smiled, however, and said, 'Good morning.'

Debbie curtly nodded and carried on eating her own breakfast.

'Debbie takes care of the boys,' Sylvester said, 'and a splendid job she's doing, too.'

This earned Sylvester a warm smile from the young woman. It was in marked contrast to the look she'd given

216

Kat. Kat wondered what she'd done to earn such dislike. Surely Debbie didn't think she was romantically involved with Sylvester? And even if she was, what on earth had it to do with the nanny? She was a pretty woman, with her blonde hair and blue eyes. She also had a good figure. Maybe she had designs on her employer. It wouldn't be the first time a man had become involved with his children's nanny, after all.

As if sensing Kat's speculation, the young woman suddenly looked up and asked, 'Are you going to be staying for long, uh, Kat?'

'No, I'm leaving right after breakfast.'

'Oh, no, please stay,' Samuel pleaded.

'I can't,' she told him with a smile. 'As much as I'd like to get to know you and Joshua, I have to go to work. I only stayed last night because I'd left my door key at my mother's and had nowhere else to go.'

Debbie's gaze was a sharp one then. 'Couldn't you have stayed at your

217

mother's? Is she local?'

'She is, but I didn't want to disturb her as she would have been in bed. And Sylvester very kindly offered me a bed here.' *And why*, she silently demanded of herself, *am I explaining myself to you?*

She couldn't mistake the other woman's expression of relief. So she was right; Debbie did have hopes for herself and Sylvester. Well, she needn't worry. The very last man Kat would let herself become involved with was Sylvester Jordan, despite last evening's shameful and wanton display.

She glanced once more at Sylvester. His eyes were gleaming with what looked once again suspiciously like amusement. She felt the skin of her face warming, which only intensified that glimmer of amusement.

'When you've had some breakfast, and before you go, Kat,' he went on to say with a completely deadpan expression — it was as if their silent exchange hadn't happened — 'there's something

I wish to discuss with you.'

'Oh?' A flicker of nervous tension made itself felt. Surely he wasn't about to mention what had happened between them — especially as he wasn't totally blameless himself. He had made a move towards her; a move that had strongly suggested he was about to kiss her. Or had she been mistaken? Had it been her intoxicated state that had led her to believe that?

'Yes. When you've eaten, come to the den. I'll see you then.'

Which very effectively deprived her of any sort of appetite at all. Clearly, he'd already eaten.

'Do you know, I think I'll skip breakfast and get off home. I'm not really very hungry.'

His gaze was a level one then. 'If you're sure?'

'I am.'

'Okay, come with me then.'

His tone was such that she didn't dare refuse, so when he led the way into a smaller room on the other side of the hallway, she meekly followed. Not before saying goodbye to the boys, however, and Debbie. Debbie again barely responded.

A feeling of deep misgiving was assailing Kat. What was coming now? If it was more about Petals and his financial offer, well, what else was there to say? Ruth had unequivocally turned him down. Still, Kat couldn't help wondering if he had something else up his sleeve, like a threat to tell Ruth where her daughter had spent the last night if she didn't persuade her mother to accept the offer. He'd most likely guessed that Ruth would be outraged at such a thing. Her heart lurched. She wouldn't put such a tactic past him. He'd demonstrated, more than once, how ruthless he could be when the occasion demanded it. Her head began to ache all over again at the mere thought of her mother knowing where she'd spent the night. She'd probably never speak to Kat again — after the initial furious outburst, naturally.

Kat glanced wildly around. Could she make a run for it? No, that would be ridiculous. She was a grown woman, for goodness sake. She'd deal with it, whatever it was he was planning to say to her.

11

However, common sense coupled with a hefty dollop of reason triumphed, and she remained where she was. What could Sylvester do, really? Cause a great deal of trouble, she counter-argued. Because if Ruth did ever find out where Kat had spent the night, then separate rooms or not, she'd definitely never speak to her daughter again. In fact, she'd be disowned right there and then.

'You mentioned last night that your catering business was struggling.'

Oh God, so she had. And with that, she recalled her fear that Sylvester might unscrupulously use that knowledge to put pressure on Ruth to accept his offer of compensation, just so she could help Kat financially.

'Well, a little, but I'm sure — '

'I want to offer you a job here at the Manor, to cook for me and the boys.

Well, for all of us, actually, Debbie and Joan included. Also, I'd like you to cater for any dinner parties I might hold. I entertain on a regular basis, sometimes — although not often — twice a week. The guests are business contacts, as well as friends. As I said before, Joan is an acceptable cook, but really she could do with concentrating on the upkeep of the house.' He cocked his head at her. 'What do you think? I'm prepared to make it worth your while financially.' He proceeded to name a salary that took Kat's breath away. 'You'd be doing me a huge favour. The job would entail working five days a week, Wednesday till Sunday, eleven to seven; later, obviously, if I'm entertaining.'

Kat didn't know what to say. A job offer was the last thing she'd expected. Of course she couldn't accept — but she had to admit, it would be a huge relief to have a regular income, especially one so generous. It would solve all of her current problems — except that of her mother, of course.

How could she possibly work on a permanent basis for the man who was trying to take her mother's home and business away, as tempting as the offer was?

'You could, of course, still cater for other people,' he went on. 'Obviously I'd have first call on your time, but if I didn't need you in the evening, well, you could do as you wished,' he suggested. 'In fact, you could even prepare some food here, in advance of any other dinner parties, to help you out. We have adequate facilities, after all.'

'I-I don't know,' she stammered. It was an irresistibly attractive proposition. She'd have to be an idiot to turn it down. Yet, the problem of how her mother would feel about her working for the enemy, as she would undoubtedly see it, was still an insurmountable one.

'Look, think about it and get back to me.'

Another problem occurred to Kat

then. 'What would Joan think about me becoming a permanent fixture?'

'Oh, she's mad keen for it to happen. I've already mentioned it to her; I wouldn't want to upset her. She's been with me for a while now. She moved back here with me, actually. I know she finds trying to keep up with the housework as well as cook for us all a bit arduous. As she frequently points out, she's not getting any younger.'

Kat hesitated, but then decided to ask the question. 'What about Debbie? How would she feel about me working here?'

He was clearly puzzled by the question, and his brow creased. 'What's it to do with Debbie? She simply cares for the boys.'

Well, that answered one question for her. It didn't sound as if there was any sort of affair going on — providing he was telling the truth, of course. She eyed him. Somehow, despite all his other faults — and they were legion in her opinion — she didn't think he'd deliberately lie. At least, not about something as innocuous as his household matters. His business dealings — well, they were a different ball game altogether.

'Okay, I'll think about it and let you know.'

'Good. I'll look forward to that. I'll take you back to your mother's.'

'No, really, I'll call a taxi. You've done more than enough for me, and — ' She felt the beginnings of a blush. ' — I'd like to apologise for-for my behaviour last night.'

'What behaviour was that then?'

'Well, you know, I-I was a bit ... well, a bit in your face, if my memory is accurate. I wouldn't want you to think that was my normal behaviour.'

'Okay. But what precisely are you talking about?'

Despite the innocent-sounding question, there was something about the manner in which he was looking at her that suggested he knew exactly what she was talking about. And yet he was obviously determined to make her spell it out. Determined to humiliate her? she wondered. It was exactly the sort of thing he'd do.

Somehow, she managed to control her vexation and ask, 'D-didn't I try t-to kiss you?'

'Oh, that.' His gaze was a level one now. 'That's my biggest regret, actually.'

'What is?' She frowned. It was her turn now to query what he was talking about.

'Well, if you hadn't had quite so much to drink and had been more aware of what it was you were offering, I might have taken you up on it. But I didn't want to be accused of sexual harassment for a second time — of taking advantage of you while you were under the influence, so to speak.'

Kat closed her eyes. Her humiliation was now complete. Trust him to spell out the exact level of her intoxication. Had the man got no compassion?

He laughed out loud suddenly. Her

eyes snapped open. 'Don't worry. It's all forgotten — well, forgiven, at any rate.'

What did that mean, forgotten or forgiven? Did he have to talk in riddles? She, for one, hadn't forgotten it, and she couldn't believe that he would have — unless it was all so unimportant on his scale of things that he hadn't given it another thought. For a moment she felt insulted, but then she recalled his words. Not taking advantage of her offer was his biggest regret, which must mean he'd wanted to. It could also mean he hadn't forgotten it either. For a second, her spirit soared.

But then he spoke, and he sounded so indifferent about everything that her heart sank to the floor. 'Are you sure I can't drive you?'

'Completely. I'll call a cab.'

★   ★   ★

She arrived back at Petals to find Ruth hard at work arranging flowers for what looked like a special order. She didn't raise her head. In fact, the atmosphere inside the small shop could best be described as glacial.

Kat stood and watched for several moments before Ruth finally looked at her. Her features were every bit as frozen as the prevailing atmosphere. Kat prepared herself for the row that now seemed inevitable. She didn't have to wait long.

'Where were you last night?' Ruth demanded to know. 'Daisy rang me to say you'd be staying at your flat, but when I rang your landline there was no reply.'

'Why didn't you ring my mobile?'

'I did, but it was obviously turned off.'

'Oh, that's right, it was. I'd forgotten I'd done that.' She paused, gathering what courage she had in the face of what she knew was inevitable before saying, 'I wasn't at my flat because I'd stupidly left my key here, so I couldn't get in.' Her words petered out. She'd have to tell her mother the truth, all of it: that she'd stayed at Linford Manor, and that Sylvester had offered her a job. She plunged onward, deciding that the sooner she got it over with the better.

'I spent the night at Linford Manor.'

It was as if she'd waved some sort of wand, because Ruth instantly stopped what she was doing and stared at her daughter. 'You what? You spent the night with Sylvester Jordan?' She looked truly appalled. 'I knew from what Daisy told me that you'd had a little bit too much to drink, and that was why you were going back to yours. But you must have consumed it by the barrel-load to agree to spend the night with him instead.'

Kat was determined not to lose her temper. That would serve no useful purpose at all. In fact, it would do the very opposite. They'd end up in a shouting match, and that would achieve nothing. 'I couldn't see I had a choice. And I didn't spend the night with him. I spent it in one of the guest bedrooms.

He-he was very kind.'

'*How* kind, exactly?' spat Ruth.

'He was courteous and considerate, and very proper. Daisy clearly told you I'd had a little too much to drink, but it definitely wasn't a barrel-load. However, knowing your views on over-indulging, I didn't think I'd be particularly welcome back here.'

Ruth was still staring at her, her eyes chips of ice. 'So what happened between the two of you?'

'I've just told you,' Kat patiently said. 'I spent the night in a guest bedroom.'

'Yes, yes.' Impatiently Ruth waved the rose she was still holding. 'But before he took you to the guest bedroom.'

'Nothing. He showed me to the room and he went to his own room, I presume.'

'You presume?' Ruth snorted with derision. 'You know he has a very attractive woman living there with him?'

'If you mean Joan, I wouldn't call her attractive.' She was being deliberately provocative, she knew, but she couldn't help herself. Ruth was behaving like a Victorian parent.

'No, no.' Ruth waved her hands about as if a swarm of angry bees were attacking her. 'The nanny. Debbie someone-or-other. It's common knowledge she doesn't just look after the children. Sylvester Jordan, by all accounts, is a serial adulterer. So it wouldn't be surprising if he also sleeps with his sons' nanny. No wonder his poor wife left him.'

Kat laughed. 'By whose account is he a serial adulterer?'

Ruth shrugged. 'Everyone's.'

'That's nothing more than spiteful gossip. Oh, for heaven's sake,' she then cried in exasperation, 'this is all too ridiculous. He's not a serial adulterer.'

'He's fooled you too, then. Well, why am I surprised?'

'He's not like that, Mum.' What the hell was she doing defending him? For all she knew, the rumours could be true. She had no proof that they were wrong, just her own gut feeling and her own experience with him. 'He was a perfect gentleman, and his two boys are gorgeous.'

'Oh, so you've met them?' Ruth did look genuinely surprised at that.

'Yes, this morning. I also met Debbie, and I don't think for a second there's anything going on with her.'

'Oh, well,' Ruth scoffed, 'you always were gullible. I mean, look what Max was up to all through your marriage. You were totally oblivious.'

'I know, but I trusted him — wrongly as it turned out,' Kat calmly said. 'I've learned better since then.'

'In that case, prove it and stay away from Sylvester Jordan.'

'He's back, actually,' Kat blurted.

'Who's back?' Ruth regarded her as if she were speaking in tongues.

'Max.'

'You're kidding!'

'No, I saw him in the pub the other night. He's single again.'

'I do hope you aren't considering taking him back. Though the way you've been behaving lately, I wouldn't be surprised.'

'Of course I'm not,' Kat indignantly repudiated the suggestion. However, the news had done what she'd hoped it would: it had successfully distracted Ruth from the topic of Sylvester. So much so, that now might be a good time to break the rest of it. 'I've got other fish to fry.'

'Please, tell me the other fish doesn't go by the name of Sylvester Jordan.'

'He's offered me a job.'

Ruth was beginning to look confused. 'Who has? Max?'

'No, Sylvester. He's asked me to cook for him at the house five days a week, Wednesday to Sunday, eleven o'clock till seven.'

'Tell me you've said no.'

'I haven't said anything yet.'

'You can't be seriously considering accepting! You'd actually work for that man?'

'For heaven's sake, will you stop referring to him as 'that man'? He's offering a fantastic salary. It would solve all of my financial problems.'

'No. No, I won't have it.'

'It's not your decision to make, Mum,' Kat quietly said. 'I've got no bookings for the foreseeable future and my bills are mounting up. I can't go on like this. I have to do something.'

'But not something for him, Kat,' Ruth wailed. 'For God's sake, you just can't — not after all he's done to me!'

'I can, and I'm going to. And we don't know that he's the one behind all the trouble.' And just like that, she made up her mind. In the end it had been relatively easy, mainly because she couldn't see any other viable option. 'I'll still come back here each evening if you want me to.'

'I don't!' Ruth cried. 'I can manage. I don't want a potential spy living here.'

Kat burst out laughing. 'Don't be ridiculous. Me, a spy?'

'It's not ridiculous. You've sided with him. That's all I need to hear.' She

turned back to her flower arrangements. 'Please go.'

Kat retreated to the flat above the
shop, as furious with her mother as her
mother was with her. Ruth had more or
less called her a traitor. Well if that was
the way she wanted things to be, then
so be it. Kat could be every bit as
stubborn as Ruth. She'd return to her
own place immediately, and then she'd
ring Sylvester and tell him she'd take
the job . . . or maybe wait another day.
She didn't want to sound too eager.

*　*　*

Sylvester sounded genuinely pleased
when Kat told him her decision. 'When
can you start?' was his first question.

'Well, tomorrow would be good.'

'Excellent.'

'It's not too soon?'

'Heavens, no. The sooner the better,
as far as I'm concerned.'

*　*　*

And that was that. Now all Kat had to do was tell Daisy that she wouldn't be needing her again. Oh Lord, what on earth would she say? She'd relied on the money she earned from Kat's catering business to supplement her income, and Kat did feel she was letting her friend down.

Oh well, best get it over with. She punched out Daisy's number on her phone and, when her friend answered, launched into an explanation of what had happened. 'I'm so sorry, Daisy, but I can't afford to turn the job down. I've been struggling, as you know . . . '

'That's okay,' Daisy said. 'I've been expecting it, actually, and I understand. But if you ever need me again, well, you know where I am — and keep in touch. You are my best friend.'

Kat felt immensely relieved at how well Daisy had taken her news. She was also relieved when Joan, too, appeared delighted the following day when Kat showed up at Linford Manor. 'What a relief it will be not to have to do all the cooking,' were her first words.

Debbie's reception of her was less encouraging, however. There was no welcoming smile, and her curt 'hello' was decidedly unwelcoming, resurrecting memories of Joan's initially hostile reception of her. As for the two little boys, they displayed contrasting emotions. Samuel was delighted and didn't try to hide it. All he seemed concerned with was whether she would cook fish fingers for their lunch.

'I think I can manage that,' she assured him with a warm smile.

'Oh, good,' he replied, 'because Joan always, always burns them.' He bestowed a comically severe glance upon the grinning housekeeper.

Joshua, on the other hand, provided a much more subdued greeting. His first words were, 'Does Mummy know you're here?'

Kat slanted a glance at Joan, desperately seeking some sort of guidance as to how to respond to the boy. She simply shrugged, obviously as much at a loss as Kat.

Kat did the best she could under the circumstances and said, 'I don't know, Joshua. You'll have to ask your daddy.'

Debbie interrupted at that point. 'Don't worry, Josh. I'm sure Daddy will tell her.'

'Will she mind?' The little boy looked quite desperately worried. 'I don't want her to be cross.'

'She won't be cross with you,' the nanny told him. She looked at Kat. 'He does worry so,' she murmured. 'He's such a sensitive boy. Of course, it doesn't help when someone new arrives.'

Kat felt that this was in some way all her fault, and she belatedly wondered if that had been Debbie's intention. She decided to make it all a little clearer. 'I'm not going to be living here, Joshua. I'll just be coming to cook for you all. It's to help Joan. She has such a lot to do. I won't be interfering in your and Samuel's lives.'

Joan smiled and said, 'That's right,

Josh. I do really need some help. I'm not getting any younger, as I keep telling you all. Now, who's for a glass of milk and a biscuit?'

'Yes, please,' Samuel sang out. Joshua, on the other hand, remained silent.

Once Debbie and the boys had gone again, Joan said, 'Josh was beside himself when his mother left. He didn't understand what was happening, bless him. He was worried it was because of him and kept asking if he'd been a naughty boy. I'd hear him crying himself to sleep every night. It was awful; heartbreaking.'

'But he sees his mother, doesn't he?'

'Not often, no; and afterward he's always very subdued — troubled, I suppose. Between you and me,' Joan added, lowering her voice, 'I think she tells him it's all his father's fault she left. That he didn't love her enough. All nonsense, of course. I was working for the family when it all started to go wrong. Well, if I'm truthful, it started long before that.' Her voice dropped even lower, so much so that Kat had to strain to hear her words. 'She was a right madam; led Mr Sylvester a proper dance. Always off out somewhere, doing Lord knows what. She left in the end with an older man; a richer man. Mind you, I don't know how Mr Sylvester put up with it as long as he did. Well,' she sniffed, 'actually I do. It was for the sake of the two boys. He didn't want them to suffer. But as you can see, it's really unsettled poor Joshua. He worries constantly that someone else will come along and replace his mother.'

Kat's heart ached for the little boy, and for Sylvester. His son's anxieties must deeply trouble him.

★   ★   ★

It didn't take long for Kat to settle into her new job. She and Joan got along splendidly, and Sylvester proved a surprisingly considerate employer. The money she received also proved a huge help. It meant she could settle her outstanding bills.

Even Joshua was warming to her, which was very encouraging. He and Samuel would often wander into the kitchen if Debbie was occupied elsewhere. They liked to help if they could with small tasks. Kat welcomed this and went out of her way to encourage them, Joshua in particular. He was growing very adept at making gingerbread men as well as eating them.

She received the impression, however, that Debbie didn't care for the growing affection between the three of them, mainly because every chance she had she insinuated that there was no need for Kat to be there. 'I could have helped Joan,' was her chief grumble, 'if someone had just asked.' Fortunately, no one took any notice. Joan would occasionally glance Kat's way in the wake of a particularly resentful remark, her gaze twinkling with amusement.

Not surprisingly, the first couple of

weeks flew by. There hadn't, as yet, been any dinner parties, so she quickly developed her own daily routine. She'd heard nothing from Ruth, which was beginning to bother her; they'd never gone this long not speaking to each other. Nevertheless, she'd decided to allow her mother a little more time to get over the anger that had consumed her upon hearing of Kat's new job. She'd always taken a while to recover from any sort of disagreement or row, whoever it was with. There was one reassuring aspect to the whole debacle: there couldn't have been any further trouble at the shop, because row or not, Ruth would undoubtedly have been on the phone to Kat.

* * *

It was the middle of the following week that Sylvester announced to Kat, 'I'm planning a dinner party for eight people, business colleagues and their wives or partners. I thought this coming

Saturday. I know it's short notice, but is that acceptable for you?'

'Of course. It's a large part of why I'm here, after all.'

He eyed her, his expression one of uncertainty. It was the first time she'd glimpsed that in him and it surprised her. As she'd said, catering dinner parties for him was part of the reason for his employing her. 'Um, I wondered if you'd join us as you did last time?'

'Oh, well . . . ' She didn't know what to say. She hadn't anticipated being a guest at the meals.

'Joan has agreed that, as well as giving a hand with the preparations, she'll also serve and clear. And . . . I'd also like it if you could stay the night. You could use the room you had the last time. That way, you wouldn't have to worry about drinking and driving.'

She stared at him. Surely he wasn't implying that she was a regular heavy drinker? That there could possibly be a repetition of the evening when she'd had too much wine?

She had her mouth open ready to repudiate such an insulting insinuation, when he chuckled with amusement. 'Don't look at me like that. I'm not suggesting that you're a habitual drinker. I simply don't want you rushing off back to your mother's.'

Yet again he'd read her mind, something he seemed able to do with troubling frequency. 'That won't be happening,' Kat muttered. 'I'm not staying with her at the moment.'

'Oh?' His one eyebrow shot up. It seemed a favourite trick of his. Maybe he was aware of the attractively rakish look it bestowed. 'Trouble?'

'A little.' She was reluctant to say any more. She didn't want him to know they'd argued about him.

But Sylvester wasn't about to let her get away with that. 'Is it about me, about you working here?'

She couldn't meet his suddenly piercing look. 'Yes,' she mumbled.

'Oh dear. Collaborating with the enemy, is that how she views it?'

'Yes.'

'Aah.' He studied her in silence. 'Has there been any further trouble at the shop?'

'I-I don't know. I don't think so. She'd have been in touch.'

He looked troubled by what she was telling him. 'It's really not me behind it all, Kat. And I'm quite sure Brett wouldn't have initiated such behaviour, either. It has to have been local lads up to mischief. It's the only explanation.'

'But we only ever saw one person.' She wrinkled her brow. 'And why would whoever it was — is — pick on Petals? All right, Charlie's was vandalised last time, but that was the only time. And another thing — the empty shops weren't damaged, not once, and if it was someone just out for mischief, they would be, surely? No, it has to be someone who wants my mother and Charlie out. And I'm sorry, but as I see it, who else can it be other than someone who works for you?'

Sylvester stared at her, his expression

a grim one. 'If it is someone who works for me, I can't think who it could be. Who would embark on such a campaign on their own initiative?'

'An employee, fearful for his job if the development doesn't go ahead?'

He frowned.

'Would you lay off people if you can't begin work?'

'Possibly. But there's no plan for that at the moment. Mind you, once the job they're on now is completed, and if we can't go ahead with Paradise Road, well . . . ' He shrugged. 'Even so, there's no excuse for such behaviour. But more to the point, in my opinion that sort of intimidation simply hardens people's resistance, and that's the last thing we need.' He gave a rueful smile. 'Though I have to say, your mother's resistance is already rock solid. She's one very determined lady.' He looked thoughtful then. 'I'll make enquiries discreetly, and if it is one of my employees I'll take immediate action, you have my word.'

12

That evening, Kat's mobile phone rang just as she was entering her flat.

'Kat, it's me, Max.'

'What do you want?' she bluntly demanded.

'You,' he equally bluntly replied.

Kat frowned. If she recalled correctly, that was what he'd said in the pub the other evening. Did he really think she'd fall for his glib words? He hadn't wanted her all the time she was married to him. Oh, he'd gone through the motions, but in truth he'd wanted someone else. In fact, looking back upon events now, she couldn't understand why he'd married her in the first place. Maybe because she'd so obviously adored him? Max had always been a sucker for a woman's — any woman's — adoration. He'd thrived upon it.

She recalled a party they'd attended not long after they'd married, where a young, attractive woman — she couldn't remember her name, but she couldn't have been much more than eighteen — had made no secret of her admiration of him. He'd stayed at her side for the better part of the evening, talking, flirting, fetching her drinks. Kat should have seen the warning signs then, but she hadn't. She'd blindly made excuses for him. He hadn't wished to be rude, hadn't wanted to hurt the young woman's feelings. When Kat tentatively brought the matter up later at home, he'd echoed her sentiments exactly. And she'd believed him. How could she have been so naive, so gullible, so trusting?

But she was no longer that young woman. Now she bluntly said, 'Well, sad to say, you can't have me.'

'Kat, Kat, please, meet me for a drink. Let's talk. Hear what I have to say, at least. I-I've missed you.'

'Huh!'

'I have, really. I'd give anything to be able to undo what I did. I want us to try again.'

Kat didn't know what to say, so she said nothing.

'Kat, are you still there?'

'Yeah, okay. Where?'

'The Green Frog, eight o'clock.'

'Okay.'

She thrust the phone back into her bag. What was he up to? And, in heaven's name, why had she agreed to go? Hadn't he hurt her enough? What was she, some sort of masochist? She resolved to be on her guard. For Max still possessed that particular brand of charm, the one that had kept her in thrall to him throughout almost all of their marriage. The one that was the reason she'd steered well clear of attractive, charmingly plausible men ever since. Men like Sylvester Jordan. Till now, that was.

And now here she was, actually working for the biggest charmer of all.

Because despite her dislike of what she still suspected he was doing to her mother and Charlie, she couldn't deny his sexual magnetism. Just as she couldn't deny how deeply she was attracted to him. And that was an appalling admission to have to make, even to herself.

She sighed and went into her bedroom to change out of her working clothes. She'd go casual; she didn't want Max thinking she was making any sort of effort for him. After opting for a pair of very ordinary denims and an equally ordinary sweater, she left the flat for the pub, where, to her astonishment, she found Max already there. He'd always been late, even on their first few dates. It was as if he'd had to prove that she'd wait for him, however long he took to get there. And of course, as head over heels in love as she'd been, she'd waited.

'Hi.' He got to his feet and leaned forward to kiss her. Kat instinctively jerked away. He took the hint — again, uncharacteristically — and asked, 'Your usual red wine?'

Something made her say, 'No. Soda water with lime, please.' A desire not to be predictable, maybe? To show she wasn't the woman he'd left behind him?

He cocked his head at her. 'On the wagon?'

'No, I just don't feel like drinking wine.' She could have added, *I want to keep my wits about me and not succumb to your practised charm*, but she didn't. It might bestow the impression that given time, he could win her back into his arms and his bed. And she was determined that that was not going to happen. Not in a million years.

'Have you eaten?' he then asked. 'I was going to order the special.'

'I've had something.' She had, in fact, eaten with Sylvester, Joan and the boys. It had been Debbie's evening off and she'd gone out. The fact that it had been just the five of them had imbued the meal with a homely, intimate feel.

So much so, that Samuel had said, 'We're a family, aren't we, Daddy? Kat can be Mummy.'

Sylvester had smiled at his son but had almost at once looked at Joshua. The boy was frowning down into his meal. He said, 'Well, I don't know what Kat would think about that, Sam.' He'd then glanced across the table at Kat, his expression a troubled one.

Kat had remained silent throughout this, a silence that was interrupted when Joshua unexpectedly said, 'That'd be nice,' before giving her a shy smile. 'It would be nice to have a mummy again.'

Kat had felt the sting of tears as pity for the motherless boy engulfed her. She stared helplessly at him before shifting her gaze to Sylvester. But Sylvester was once again watching his oldest son.

'Joshua, you have a mummy already.'

'I know, Daddy, but I never see her. I want another one, one who'll stay here with us.'

Now Sylvester did look at Kat, and his smile was every bit as shaky as his son's had been. He mouthed, 'Sorry.'

Kat softly said, 'Don't be. I understand.'

'You won't leave, will you, Kat?' Joshua asked.

She was stunned. What the hell was she expected to say to that? 'Um, well,' she stumbled as she frantically searched for the right words, 'I-I don't have any plans to do so at the moment. I love cooking for you all.'

'Kat has her own home, Josh,' Sylvester said, obviously taking pity on her, caught as she was in such a difficult moment. 'But we all hope she'll stay with us.' He then gave a crooked smile and added, 'Her cooking's fab. We've never eaten so well. I'll soon be so fat I won't be able to move.' And he rubbed at his stomach, at the same time puffing out his cheeks.

His light words and comical actions effectively eased the growing tension in the room, and they'd all laughed.

Especially when Joan chipped in, 'Well, I for one hope she'll stay. I'm thoroughly enjoying the break from cooking; and I agree, her cooking's fab.'

Kat watched Max go to the bar now, and all of a sudden found herself wishing it was Sylvester with her. She'd make no protest if he tried to kiss her. Oh God, what was happening to her? She felt her face growing hot and her heartbeat quickening as realisation struck her.

No, no, she hadn't, had she? She couldn't have been that stupid. But, too late, she knew she had. She was in love, deeply in love, head over heels in love, with Sylvester Jordan.

She became aware of Max sitting down by the side of her once more. He handed her the drink she'd requested. 'Please, Kat, can't we try again? I've changed, really I have.'

'So have I, and I'm sorry, but I've moved on.' Oh boy, and how she'd moved on. She'd only gone and fallen for another charmer. Still, it gave her the strength to resist any blandishment that Max might make. 'I'm not at all the person I was.'

'I can see that. You've grown much more beautiful. Makes me even more certain that I made a gigantic mistake.' He slanted a quizzical gaze at her. 'Is your refusal to give me a second chance anything to do with the things I've heard?'

'I don't know.' Her heart performed a somersault of apprehension. 'What have you heard?'

'That you're working for the man who's trying to kick your mother out of her shop and home — the notorious Sylvester Jordan.'

Kat didn't answer him. He was making it sound like the worst kind of betrayal, just like Ruth had.

'I'll take your silence for a yes, shall I?'

She shrugged and picked up her glass of tonic water, suddenly wishing it was red wine. It would have helped her get through this inquisition. 'I need the money,' she managed to say, though that was hardly any sort of justification for what could be interpreted as treachery. She wondered how many others were thinking the same — that she'd betrayed her mother.

'So you're not attracted to him then?'

She gave what she hoped was an incredulous laugh. 'Of course not.'

He eyed her, not speaking for a moment. 'Is the catering not going well? Is that why you've gone to work for him?'

'It's only temporary. It's a quiet period. I'm sure it'll soon improve.'

'Are you? Maybe other people are thinking the same as me — that you've let your mother down. Have you thought of that?'

She hadn't, actually, not till a couple of seconds ago. Her spirits sank. Could that be what was happening; why she wasn't getting any bookings? Maybe rumours had got around, and prospective clients had judged her and found her wanting. No, that was silly. She'd had no bookings even before she'd gone to work for Sylvester.

'How could you work for such a man?' Max petulantly burst out. 'I've been asking around and he's being labelled a heartless entrepreneur; a hatchet man.'

'Really? I thought everyone wanted this development. That's what I've been told.'

'Who by? The great man himself?' He arched an eyebrow at her. 'What else would he say, Kat? Honestly, I didn't have you down as that gullible.'

'Why not? I thought that was exactly what you had me down as. After all, I believed everything you told me.'

He fell silent then, before clearly deciding to change tack away from himself and his betrayal of her. 'What does your mum think of your new job?'

'It's nothing to do with her.'

'I'd have thought it had a great deal to do with her. It's tantamount to dining with the enemy — literally, in your case.'

She got to her feet. She didn't have to sit here and put up with this. 'I didn't meet you to have to listen to this. And I don't think you've got any room to criticise me for betraying my mum, do you?'

Max also got to his feet. 'I'm sorry, Kat. It's none of my business.'

'That's right, it isn't. So I think I'll leave. This is going nowhere.'

'I'll walk back with you. I presume you walked.'

'Yes, and I'll go alone, thank you.'

'Kat, please.' He did seem genuinely anguished.

But Kat hardened her heart and turned away, resolutely making her way towards the exit. Max had always been able to assume the most appropriate expression in order to manipulate her. Well, he wasn't going to do it this time. She kept walking. Undaunted, he followed her outside and then along the road.

'I can't let you go like this. I'm serious, Kat — I want you back. I still love you. I never stopped.' He grabbed hold of her by the one arm and pulled her back, turning her to face him. 'And I think — no, hope — you still love me.'

'Max, I don't. Now please, let me go.'

But he took no notice. He yanked her against him and roughly kissed her.

Kat, taken by surprise, froze, not knowing how to react. She didn't want to make an exhibition of herself on the street; she'd already done that once, according to Sylvester at least. So instead of struggling against his tight grip, she stood perfectly still, making no response at all, hoping he'd take the hint and release her.

He didn't, and so neither of them noticed Sylvester.

Once again, he was driving by and saw what was happening. His expression hardened and his eyes darkened, but although he slowed, he didn't stop. Instead, he toed the accelerator and sped onward. So he didn't see, just a couple of seconds later, Max releasing her. She immediately walked away, leaving him gazing after her, his expression one of resigned acceptance.

★ ★ ★

The next morning Kat arrived at Linford Manor earlier than usual. She wanted to start preparations for tomorrow evening's dinner party. Sylvester had left the menu to her to decide, so having written out her choice of ingredients, she'd picked them up on her way. It meant she and Joan could get started immediately.

However, when she got to the kitchen, there was no sign of the housekeeper, or anyone else for that matter. She began unpacking the shopping and was almost finished when Sylvester strode into the room.

'Good morning,' he curtly said. 'You're early. Good.'

His expression, when she swivelled to look at him, was a formidable one. A tremor of misgiving went through her. Someone had clearly upset him. She hoped it wouldn't turn out to be her.

But that hope swiftly proved a vain one. 'I saw you last evening,' he said.

'Did you? Where?' An even deeper sense of misgiving made itself felt.

'Outside the Green Frog, making an exhibition of yourself again, with your ex.' He ground out the last word, his eyes glittering with an expression she was having trouble identifying. 'I saw you once before, kissing another man. Tell me, how many men do you have dancing attendance on you?'

'None, actually,' she angrily retaliated. 'And if you'd lingered instead of leaping to conclusions, you'd have seen me walking away from him.' Though why she was explaining — excusing herself to him — she couldn't have said. It was none of his business whom she kissed. He had no right to judge her, none at all. Not with his reputation. Anyway, she was nothing to him, other than an employee.

But then something changed in his

expression. 'And why was that? Did he not satisfy you?'

'That's none of your damned business,' she cried, translating her thoughts of just a moment ago into words, regardless of whatever consequences she might be inviting. Namely, that of losing her job. 'And how come *you* were out last night? As I recall, Debbie had the evening off, so who was with the boys?'

'Joan. She usually stands in for Debbie if I need to go out. I had been to your flat to find you.'

'To find me? Why? To ask me how many men I intend to make love to? The answer to that is a simple one: none. In fact, I'm done with the entire male population. You can't trust any of them.' She did briefly feel a little guilty at lumping Ben in with that verdict. After all, he'd done nothing wrong, other than attempt to make her love him.

Sylvester's lips quirked at the corners as if he were rigorously suppressing some sort of emotion. 'Really? None of us?'

She could see now that it was amusement he was trying so hard to suppress. Indignation surged within her. He thought she was funny, did he? It wasn't the first time. 'That's right, not one of you,' she said. 'In my experience, you're all only after one thing.'

'Are we?' He continued to scrutinise her. 'In that case, I won't ask you what that one thing is. But just to make things clear, I didn't have any sort of ulterior motive. I tried to find you because I wanted to discuss Joshua's remarks about you being another mother. I didn't want you scared away by too many demands being placed on you.'

'Believe me, it would take more than one child's remarks to scare me away from anything. He misses his mother. It's perfectly natural.'

'Well I'm glad to hear you're not easily scared, because we like having you around.'

264

'Even you?' she scornfully asked.

'Especially me,' he softly said.

Completely unnoticed by Kat, he'd once again managed to inch closer to her. Startled by this unexpected proximity, she stared up at him, her eyes wide and luminous. A mixture of exasperation with him and quivering desire made her breath catch in her throat. How did he manage to move so close, completely unnoticed by her?

'Kat,' he murmured hoarsely, 'you'll have to stop looking at me like that.'

She couldn't help herself whispering, 'Or what?'

He didn't say anything for an endless moment. Then he groaned, 'Or this,' and he wrapped both his arms about her, pulling her against him as he lowered his head to hers. The kiss that followed took Kat's breath away. It was passionate, but at the same time rough, definitely sexy, and Sylvester wasn't making any attempt to conceal his passion for her. His hands reached down and pressed her even closer, making it feel as if their bodies were one. She felt a warmth begin deep within her as his hands moved, sliding up and around to caress her breasts, before dropping again to encircle her waist and then slipping on down, back over her hips. Her hands moved too, up over his chest and broad shoulders, until finally her fingers entwined at the nape of his neck. They slid in amongst his silky strands of hair. She heard him moan deep in his throat as his lips ground over hers, forcing them apart to allow his tongue to slide sensuously inside.

'Oh God,' he moaned, 'I've never felt so — '

Suddenly the door to the kitchen opened. They sprang apart like two guilty children.

Joan stood there, her face alight with good-natured amusement and some-thing else, something that looked remarkably like satisfaction. 'Sorry to interrupt,' she said. 'I just came to get these.' She picked up a couple of dusters from the worktop before hurrying out once more.

Sylvester and Kat regarded each other, Kat's face flushed with pink, Sylvester's the colour of skimmed milk. He looked every bit as shaken as she was, but he still managed to respond to her embarrassed grin. 'A timely interruption I think,' he murmured with belated and maddening composure.

Kat could only assume he was relieved that things had so abruptly been ended. Disappointment mingled with outrage swamped her. How could he be so cool, so unmoved, in the aftermath of their kiss?

But then he added throatily, 'The kitchen isn't where I'd planned for that to happen.'

Kat could have jumped for joy. So he wasn't regretting it. That knowledge emboldened her sufficiently for her to ask, 'Oh, where had you planned it, then?'

But maddeningly, before he could respond the door opened again and

Debbie, Josh and Sam walked in. Debbie took in the scene at a glance and her expression darkened dramatically. There was no mistaking her feelings about what she sensed had just taken place between the two people standing so close together.

Sylvester, clearly not noticing this, glanced back at Kat and mouthed, 'Later?'

Kat, overwhelmed with joy, nodded. Later? She couldn't wait.

13

But things didn't turn out quite as Kat had hoped, because when she asked Joan how many there would be for the evening meal, Joan replied, 'Well, Mr Sylvester's had to go out on a last-minute engagement, and I'm meeting a friend for a bite to eat, so it'll just be the boys and Debbie — unless you're staying?'

'Oh, no, I won't be staying.'

Now that there was no hope of seeing Sylvester, the very last person she wanted to dine with was Debbie, even in the company of the boys. Ever since the nanny had walked into the kitchen and picked up on the emotional vibes between her employer and Kat, she'd gone out of her way to make things as uncomfortable for Kat as she could. Her remarks, already heavy with jealousy and resentment, grew even more barbed, more weighted with hostility — all of which ensured that Kat went to great lengths to avoid her whenever possible. It wasn't easy, even in a house the size of the Manor.

So Kat spent a quiet and dispirited evening alone in her flat. She mustered the courage to call her mother, hoping she'd be able to put things right between them. As much as Ruth could infuriate her at times, Kat didn't like being at odds with her, not for any length of time. But Ruth had been pointedly unforthcoming, answering each of Kat's questions and remarks with single-word responses. Eventually Kat had given up and resigned herself to the prospect of their rift continuing for a while yet. But at least Ruth had admitted, when pressed, that there'd been no further trouble, so Kat took some consolation from that.

With the awkward phone call over, her thoughts reverted to Sylvester. She was tormented with disturbing images of him with a woman: having dinner, making love. She abandoned her efforts to watch TV and went to bed, where she spent a practically sleepless night.

* * *

Saturday dawned, the day of Sylvester's dinner party. Kat was undecided, in the wake of his unexplained absence the evening before, as to whether to join the guests or not. His teasing promise of 'later' hadn't materialised into any sort of liaison, romantic or otherwise, and her disappointment remained agonisingly acute.

However, she had far too much to do to dwell on Sylvester's broken promise. Maybe he'd simply changed his mind, or decided he'd overstepped the mark. She resolved to put the entire episode out of her mind — as possibly he already had — and get on with what needed to be done. And she almost succeeded. Only the occasional, fleeting thought of him interrupted her preparations, though each time it did she was left feeling depressed and desperately miserable.

Joan was a willing helper, and so everything was ready by six thirty. The cold starters had been placed on the table, the main course was in the warming oven along with the vegetables, and a selection of desserts was waiting on the kitchen worktop along with a cheese board.

'You go and get changed,' Joan told her. 'The guests are arriving at seven thirty. You're in the same bedroom as last time.'

Kat had changed her mind about staying for dinner and spending the night. But supposing Sylvester had another woman coming to join him for the meal? she couldn't help but wonder. He'd hardly welcome Kat's presence as well. For one thing, it would make an uneven number of guests; something which he didn't welcome, seeing as that had been the reason he'd asked her to join the first dinner party she'd catered for him. Yet he had asked her to stay.

Still deeply unsure whether she was doing the right thing, Kat fetched her overnight bag from her van. She'd carefully arranged the dress she'd found the time to buy especially for the occasion between layers of tissue paper, ensuring it didn't get creased. She pulled it out now and held it up in front of her. It was midnight-blue, sleek and figure-hugging, with a low neckline and subtly freckled with the occasional sequin.

Once she had it on, she eyed her reflection in the full-length mirror. The dress clung and moulded itself to every one of her curves. What would Sylvester think? She'd bought it with him in mind, but now she wasn't sure that it had been the right choice. Would he see it as deliberately provocative? An invitation? There was a considerable amount of creamy flesh on display, flesh that was enhanced by the deep shade of the dress. She frowned. If only he'd kept his promise the night before, she'd at least know now where she stood with him. And, more to the point, whether she was being a complete fool or not.

She shrugged and turned from the mirror. It was too late to do anything about it in any case. The dress would have to do. She didn't have time to return home and find something else.

But she needn't have worried. Sylvester's expression as she walked into the sitting room told her all she so desperately wanted to know. A tiny flame flickered in the depths of his eyes, illuminating what looked dangerously like desire as his gaze raked her from the top of her artfully piled-up hair down to the tips of her high-heeled shoes.

'You look gorgeous,' he huskily murmured. 'Tasty enough to eat.'

Kat blushed hotly.

'Oh God, and she blushes too. I'd forgotten that,' he muttered, for all the world as if he were in the most acute anguish. 'What's a man to do?' he concluded helplessly.

But sadly she had no time to discover

the answer to that intriguing question, because the first of the guests walked into the room. Within another ten minutes everyone was there, so Kat and Sylvester had no time to say any more.

It didn't stop her from shivering with delicious anticipation, though. They'd have to wait till everyone had gone. She shivered again. Maybe he'd kiss her? If he didn't, she was sure she'd die.

★   ★   ★

The evening passed with maddening slowness. Even so, Kat thrilled every time Sylvester's smouldering glance rested upon her, which it did with noticeable and increasing frequency.

After what felt like an eternity to Kat, but in reality was a mere three and a half hours, they bade farewell to the last couple and, with Joan long since gone to bed, they were finally alone.

Without saying a word, Sylvester poured them both a brandy and handed Kat a glass. 'The food was exquisite,' he told her, 'as are you.' Once again he let his gaze roam lazily over her, lingering on the spot where her shadowy cleavage showed, and making no attempt to hide his desire. He placed his glass on the nearby low table and removed hers from her hand. He then led her to one of the three huge settees and gently pushed her down onto it before following suit himself.

'There's something I want to tell you,' he said. He looked unaccountably nervous all of a sudden, and he'd left a gap of at least twelve inches between them.

Kat's heart spiralled into a nosedive. What was he going to say? That there could never be anything between them? He had to think of the boys, put them first?

But no. He leaned across to her and pulled her close. He then wrapped both arms around her. He didn't kiss her, however, but simply gazed deeply into her troubled eyes.

'I know you regard me as a greedy,

unscrupulous businessman who'll stop at nothing to get what he wants, even if that includes forcing two people from their homes. But I've come up with an idea. A possible solution.'

Kat's disappointment then knew no bounds. Here she'd been expecting him to make love to her; instead, he wished to talk business. She pulled sharply away.

'No, don't,' he muttered. 'Just hear me out. I have something to say first.'

'Okay.'

'I'm going to retain ownership of the new store, so that means I'm in a position to offer Ruth and Charlie space for their businesses on mutually agreed terms. They'll still get all the money I've offered as compensation for lost trade while the building work's being done. It'll mean they don't have to move into another area and so, hopefully, not lose their regular customers, and it would also mean they could buy themselves new homes with the money they'll receive. There should be more than enough. I've just completed a terrace of one-bedroom houses in Nobleton. They could each have one of those. They wouldn't be far from the store and their shops, three or four miles at most. They're also very competitively priced as starter homes. They can even rent those if that's what they prefer. I don't know why I didn't think of it before.' He looked anxiously at her. 'So what do you think? Would they go for it? It would solve the problem and clear the way, hopefully, for us to-to — '

'To — ?' Her heart pounded ferociously; her breathing quickened in feverish anticipation.

'To start a new life together. I love you, Kat; I have from the first moment I saw you again. I-I hope you feel the same way.' Again, he looked very unsure of himself.

As for Kat, what he was saying was the very last thing she'd expected to hear. She stared at him, her eyes wide and luminous.

'I'm asking you to marry me, Kat. The boys would love it, both of them, as I'm sure you know. So would Joan.'

'What about Debbie?' she couldn't resist asking. 'I have a feeling she won't be so pleased.'

'She'll have to deal with it. She'll come round.' Clearly he too had noticed the younger woman's resentment of Kat. 'So, what do you say?'

Kat nodded, for the moment incapable of any sort of rational dialogue. Then she managed to blurt, 'Oh God, yes, yes!'

'Oh, my darling,' he murmured, 'that's all I wanted to hear.'

He pulled her into his arms and proceeded to make love to her with all the passion and tenderness that Kat had been aching for.

Eventually he straightened up and said, 'I think we ought to go and see Ruth now. Get everything sorted out. Will she still be up?'

'Oh yes, it's only just gone eleven

thirty,' Kat eagerly replied. 'She's a night owl. I'll give her a ring.'

★ ★ ★

Minutes later, they were in Sylvester's car and on their way to Petals. Sylvester had knocked on Debbie's bedroom door and called that they were going out for a short while, thus ensuring the boys would be taken care of should they wake. Kat dreaded to think what she'd make of that.

'I usually get up in the night to them,' he'd told Kat. She hadn't been surprised. He'd proved over and over what a good father he was. He'd then slanted a glance at her and said, 'Who knows? Maybe before too long they'll have a little sister or brother.'

Kat was yet again rendered speechless.

'Would you be okay with that?' he'd then asked.

'It's what I've always wanted,' she'd said in a voice that shook.

Once they arrived in Paradise Road, as late as it was, there wasn't a parking space to be had in front of the row of shops. Sylvester parked his car a little further along the road and, hand in hand, they walked back to Petals. There was no one around, so the cars must all belong to the inhabitants of the homes that lay on one side of the road still.

They were a mere fifty metres from the shop when they noticed the darkly clad figure positioned in front of it. Kat gasped. It had to be the person responsible for all the trouble.

'Sssh,' cautioned Sylvester. 'We've got him.'

Even as they watched, the person lifted an arm into the air. He was about to throw something — a brick? Sylvester flung himself towards whoever it was. 'Got you,' he said.

There was a brief struggle as the perpetrator tried to free himself, but it was no good; Sylvester was several inches taller and much stronger.

The assailant gasped, 'Syl-Sylvester, please don't!'

Sylvester let go. 'Mother?' he shouted as he ripped the hat from her head. 'What the hell are you doing?'

And then it all came out — Maria's halting admission that it had all been down to her: the damaged windows, the phone calls, the firework.

'But why?' Sylvester demanded to know. 'Why would you do such things, for God's sake? And does Father know?'

'No, I always waited till he was going to be out late. I wanted to help you get what you needed, darling; I always have. I'm so sorry, Sylvester.' She began to weep. 'It was terribly wrong of me. Will you both forgive me?'

But Kat wasn't ready to forgive Maria for all the fear and distress she'd caused; not yet. All she said was a curt, 'We'd better go up and see my mother. She needs to know about this.'

Maria's face drained of colour, but she said nothing and made no sort of protest.

It was Ruth who truly astonished Kat. She listened to Maria's confession without displaying any of the angry outrage that Kat had expected. 'Where our children are concerned,' she calmly said, 'we'd do anything.' She was resolutely disregarding Kat's raised eyebrows. 'I won't press charges — providing, of course, it all stops now.'

'It will,' Sylvester grimly told her. 'That's why I'm here, actually. I've come up with a solution, hopefully, to our problem.'

Ruth waited expectantly, and in silence, which was definitely a first in Kat's opinion. And then, when Sylvester had told her all that he'd suggested to Kat, again to Kat's amazement Ruth accepted his offer with the proviso that both shops would be on the ground floor. 'I have to have a lot of my flowers delivered,' she explained, 'and the delivery men will need easy access to me. Charlie, I'm sure, will feel the same way. But I'm sure he'll accept it, too,' Ruth then went on. 'Truth to tell, we're both tired of the fight — Charlie certainly is — and we want matters settled. And, well, it all does sound very satisfactory; enticing, even.'

So everything was finally resolved as far as the shops were concerned. As late as it was, Charlie had also been invited in; and he too, just as Ruth had anticipated, readily agreed to the proposals.

With Charlie back in his own flat, all Sylvester and Kat had to do was break the news of their engagement. Sylvester cleared his throat and, taking hold of Kat's hand once again, said, 'We have some more news for you both.'

Ruth and Maria stared at them, and then, still in silence, looked down at their joined hands. Ruth eventually said, 'I think we've probably guessed what it is. What do you say, Maria?'

Maria nodded, looking directly at Kat for the first time. 'I've been expecting it, actually. Sylvester's done nothing but talk about you.'

Ruth, not to be outdone, said, 'I'm not surprised either.'

Kat regarded her mother anxiously, but Ruth didn't look too displeased. Nevertheless, she couldn't stop herself from asking, 'Mum, are you okay with this? We really love each other, and now that we know the truth . . . ' Maria's face coloured but she stayed silent.

'Kat, I just want you to be happy. I always have,' Ruth said. 'And you obviously are. So yes, you have my blessing, both of you.'

Kat and Sylvester both looked at Maria then. 'Mum?' Sylvester said.

'Same for me. Your father will be pleased, I'm sure. Like Ruth, we want you to be happy, you and the boys.'

With that satisfactorily agreed, Kat and Sylvester returned to the manor house, Kat feeling a huge sense of relief at her mother's ready acceptance of Sylvester as her future son-in-law. Of course, Sylvester's case had probably been helped enormously by his offer to her and Charlie.

Their brandies were still awaiting them at the house, so without sitting down they quickly drank them, and then Sylvester said, 'I don't know what to say. All the time it was my mother. I can't believe it. If I'd had any idea . . . She must have been suffering from some form of lunacy.' He shook his head in disbelief. 'God knows what my father is going to say to her.'

'I'm sure they'll sort things out between them. I'm simply glad it's all cleared up.'

'And me. I feel as if a huge weight has been lifted off me.'

Kat went to him and put her arms around him. 'I'm so sorry I ever suspected you.'

'How sorry?' he teasingly asked. 'Sorry enough to fix an early wedding date?'

'Definitely. How does April sound? A spring wedding. I'm sure we'll be able to fix it.'

'I think I'll manage to wait that long.' Desire smouldered in his eyes. 'It won't be easy, but for now, well, I think we have some rather important business to finish.'

'Oh?' She glanced up at him from beneath provocatively lowered eyelids. 'What could that be?'

'This.' He lowered his head to hers, at the same time walking her backwards to the settee, whereupon he gently pushed her down onto it, and for the second time that evening proceeded to make love to her with heart-melting passion and tenderness.

We do hope that you have enjoyed reading this large print book.

Did you know that all of our titles are available for purchase?

We publish a wide range of high quality large print books including:
Romances, Mysteries, Classics
General Fiction
Non Fiction and Westerns

Special interest titles available in large print are:
The Little Oxford Dictionary
Music Book, Song Book
Hymn Book, Service Book

Also available from us courtesy of Oxford University Press:
Young Readers' Dictionary
(large print edition)
Young Readers' Thesaurus
(large print edition)

For further information or a free brochure, please contact us at:
Ulverscroft Large Print Books Ltd.,
The Green, Bradgate Road, Anstey,
Leicester, LE7 7FU, England.
Tel: (00 44) **0116 236 4325**
Fax: (00 44) **0116 234 0205**

Other titles in the
Linford Romance Library:

STORM CHASER

Paula Williams

When Caitlin Mulryan graduates from university and returns to Stargate, the small Dorset village where she grew up, she is dismayed to find that the longstanding feud between her family and the Kingtons is as fierce as ever. Soon her twin brother is hunted down in his boat *Storm Chaser* by his bitter enemy, with tragedy in their wake — and Caitlin can only blame herself for her foolish actions. So falling in love with handsome Yorkshireman Nick Thorne is the last thing on her mind . . .

THE PARADISE ROOM

Sheila Spencer-Smith

The stone hut on the cliffs holds special memories for Nicole, who once spent so many happy hours within its walls — so when she has the chance to purchase it, she is ecstatic. Then the past catches up with her when Connor, the itinerant artist she fell in love with all those years ago, reappears in her life. But has his success changed him? And what of Daniel, the charismatic sculptor she has recently met? Nicole's heart finds itself torn between past and present . . .